A Candlelight Ecstasy Romance®

"I WAS PERFECTLY ALL RIGHT," SHE SAID WITH A LITTLE TOSS OF HER HEAD.

"Says who?" he shouted as his strong arms reached out and scooped her to him in one swift motion. "Now who's going to save you?" he asked.

"Who says I want to be saved?" she whispered as suddenly her body began to sing against his and her voice grew husky with emotion. In an instant she wanted him, and now that seemed more important than anything else.

"I like that thought." His lips began to move over her features until they hungrily captured her mouth and their bodies melted into one long rapturous caress. He lifted her and easily carried her while their lips met again and again. He tightened his embrace and curved her body close to his as they moved down the hall. . . .

A CANDLELIGHT ECSTASY ROMANCE®

JUST CALL MY NAME

DOROTHY ANN BERNARD

A CANDLELIGHT ECSTASY ROMANCE®

To Our Readers:

We have been delighted with your enthusiastic response to Candlelight Ecstasy Romances®, and we thank you for the interest you have shown in this exciting series.

In the upcoming months we will continue to present the distinctive, sensuous love stories you have come to expect only from Ecstasy. We look forward to bringing you many more books from your favorite authors and also the very finest work from new authors of contemporary romantic fiction.

As always, we are striving to present the unique, absorbing love stories that you enjoy most—books that are more than ordinary romance.

Your suggestions and comments are always welcome. Please write to us at the address below.

Sincerely,

The Editors
Candlelight Romances
1 Dag Hammarskjold Plaza
New York, New York 10017

To Our Readers:

We have been delighted with your enthusiastic response to Candlelight Ecstasy Romances™, and we thank you for the interest you have shown in this exciting series.

In the upcoming months we will continue to present the distinctive sensuous love stories you have come to expect only from Ecstasy. We look forward to bringing you many more books from your favorite authors and also the very finest work from new and exciting contemporary romantic fiction.

As always, we are striving to present the unique, absorbing love stories that you enjoy most—books that are more than ordinary romance.

Your suggestions and comments are always welcome. Please write to us at the address below.

Sincerely,

The Editor
Candlelight Romances
1 Dag Hammarskjold Plaza
New York, New York 10017

CHAPTER ONE

Clayton Farley looked through his long-range binoculars and a frown played over his face. He reached for his rifle, shrugged into a rugged jacket, and plopped a hat on his head as he moved across the neat rustic living room of his snug cabin. He pulled the door closed, locking it securely, and then took another look through a telescope from the porch of his house. There was movement on the perimeter of his property more than a mile away, but he couldn't make it out other than that he was sure it had to have something to do with human activity. His blood boiled as he thought of someone invading the sanctity of his hideaway. He moved with a purposeful stride, gun in hand, toward the action. His breathing quickened as he looked up through the trees and he unconsciously savored the woodsy scent. Branches whispered past his ears as his six-foot-plus frame maneuvered through the gauntlet of foliage. His feet hit the ground solidly in sync with his feelings and his well-coordinated muscular body moved with a catlike grace, giving him the appearance of a modern-day Tarzan in rugged woodsman's clothes. But as the fragrance of the pines enveloped him and the rhythm of his rapid stride naturally tempered his fervor, his instantaneous rage of a few moments before was effectively calmed. Nevertheless this was his land and he wasn't going to tolerate intruders.

After a while, his pace having slackened considerably, he stopped and looked through the field glasses again. "My God," he exclaimed as the figure of a woman came into focus. He watched in amazement as she moved around a small cleared area with a book in her hand. She was obviously confused and apparently alone as he scanned piles of makeshift camping equipment. As he watched, everything she attempted seemed to be an indication of total ineptness. When she raised her hand to her forehead to wipe perspiration away, leaving a dirty black smudge, he took in her rumpled jeans and dwelled on the trim thrust of her breasts through a baggy T-shirt.

He moved on, shaking his head, wondering what this could be about. He stopped often now, easily adjusting his muscular stance and gazing through the binoculars in growing amusement. The confusion and frustration on her face told the whole story, but he couldn't possibly imagine what she was doing. She referred to the book constantly, and then went from one mess to another, apparently trying to establish an overnight campsite. The small pup tent lay in a shambles where she had given up on it a few moments before. Then she was busily carrying in rocks for what looked like a fire pit area when she finally realized she needed to clear away the grass. Apparently she had missed that in her instructions and now she sat looking completely dejected and exhausted as she dropped the shovel she had tried to use for that purpose.

Clay ran his hands over the angular planes of his face and squinted his eagle-sharp eyes as he sat on a rock not more than a hundred yards away and continued to watch in fascination. As his finely molded lips settled into a permanent quirk, he could see that she was a very attractive woman in her late twenties or early thirties, and the sun picked up burnished red highlights from her shoulder-length brown hair. Again he acknowledged his appreciation of her round, firm figure and felt the first stirrings of a tender amusement as he watched her with concern.

He had established that she was not on his property, but just beyond its boundary in the Ouachita National Forest, which bordered his homesite in the middle of Arkansas. Ordinarily he would just have retreated back to his well-fortified compound in these remote and primitive hills, but he knew if this woman was planning to spend the night camping she was in for a lot of trouble.

Something just seemed to draw him on. Taking a deep breath, he squared his shoulders and utilized the corded strength of his arms as he unconsciously grabbed his rifle and strode purposely into the clearing, scaring the life out of Jessica Andres. The food preparation area she was attempting to contrive between two trees came crashing down at the same time. "Oh, my God," she shouted in a complete panic. "Don't shoot me. . . . This is government land!"

Clay grimaced at her reaction, his straight nose and firm jaw lining up with the solid thrust of his chin. He

11

had completely forgotten that he was carrying a gun. "I know it's government land," he said, "and I'm not going to shoot anyone unless they come onto my property, which starts right over there." He gestured expansively and Jessica looked at him in wide-eyed disbelief.

"Well, just go back to it and leave me alone," she stammered as she immediately noticed his demanding hypnotic eyes and rustic good looks. "I'm not bothering anyone."

"It looks to me like you're having a lot of problems," he said with a little smile. "Are you planning to camp here all by yourself?"

"That's none of your business," she said warily as she instinctively responded to his husky ruggedness and moved a few steps away. There was a demanding air addled with a confusing gentleness about him that left her perplexed. Also, as she unavoidably noted how his tight jeans accentuated narrow hips, a flat stomach, and hard thighs, raw potent virility seemed to literally exude from him. It was more than a little disconcerting, to say the least.

"I understand that," he said, noting her flustered reaction, "but camping alone, especially a woman camping alone, can be dangerous. And, if you're totally inexperienced as you obviously are, it's bound to be a disaster."

"Who says I'm inexperienced," she said with a touch of hauteur as her hair tumbled over her shoulders, giving her a paradoxical air of innocent vulnerability. "Camping's no big deal. It's just a matter of reading the book and following instructions. . . ."

"What book?" he asked as he tried to stifle a smile

12

and succeeded in illuminating the squareness of his features in an appealing way.

"The Brownie and Girl Scout Handbook," she said. "You see, it's all perfectly laid out here in the chapter 'World of Outdoors.' "

"You're in real trouble, lady," he said as he feasted on the purity of her features and then glanced at the drawings and instructions. "Why don't you just take the training course the Girl Scouts give for this sort of thing?"

"I know it can't be much different from glorified playing house," she said, willing her eyes not to focus on the cleft in his chin. "And on the day of the training I had an important story assignment. . . ."

"Story?" he asked with a bit of an edge to his voice, in contrast to its deep huskiness a moment before as he moved back a step or two.

"Yes," said Jessica as she went rambling on realizing she was after all glad to see someone in this wilderness. Camping wasn't exactly as easy as she had assumed it would be. "My little girl, Janey, is a Brownie and I'm her troop leader. I promised to take the girls camping and I figured I'd better have a dress rehearsal before I gave it a shot with all twenty of them. Janey's staying with her grandmother for the weekend while I figure this out."

"You're planning to take twenty Brownies camping?" he asked incredulously.

"Yes," she said firmly as her determination and spirit were instantaneously restored by the challenge in his voice. "If you can read and it's in a book, you ought to be able to do it. I've always operated that way and this isn't going to be any different."

13

"Well, then, why don't you use a little sense?" he asked impatiently. His lips seemed to curl in a preposterous, sensuous way that accented his implications perfectly. "Go somewhere where there are rangers and a more controlled atmosphere?"

"If I'm going to do it, I want it to be the real thing," she said as she brushed her hair back and Clay again noted the free action of her breasts. "I don't want some pretend experience. I promised Janey the real thing, and that's what she's going to get."

Completely aghast now, he made no pretense of his honest skepticism as he spread his arms in a muscle-rippling expansive gesture. "Don't you understand that camping in the rough is something that takes experience? You need to hone your instincts."

"I can handle it," she said menacingly, her green eyes snapping. "Just leave me alone and I'm sure I can manage."

"You're sure about that?"

"I'm sure!"

"This I've gotta see," he said as a big grin broke out on his face. His eyes were suddenly blindingly blue and they lit up his craggy suntanned features with a new emphasis as he lifted his woodsman's hat and ruffled his abundant wavy hair with his fingers. There was an obvious air of orneriness about him as his large frame bounded back to his own property and he nonchalantly flopped onto a grassy knoll that overlooked the area where Jessica stood in outraged consternation.

"Go to hell," she shouted, as it was obvious that he meant to remain there at his leisure, watching every movement she made. "I'm going to do this," she muttered to herself, but she cursed the flush she felt creeping over her entire body as she looked up and met his laughing eyes again.

Two spots of color accented her cheeks and seemed a natural accompaniment to her angry motions as she turned her back on him. His eyelids lowered now to a sly half-mast position above a mischievous smile, Clay perused, in obvious enjoyment, the action of her trim bottom and wondered what it would look like in a bikini instead of those rumpled jeans. He was honestly fascinated and he admitted it. She was certainly being very foolish, but he liked the touch of unwarranted self-confidence and the way she tossed her head. He frankly acknowledged that it had been some time since any woman had claimed his attention to such an extent. Actually not since he had come to the cabin to live full-time.

Fleetingly a dark look passed over his face as he thought briefly of the deception that had sent him there. He remembered the trust he had placed in his partner, Clare, and the way it had been returned when she blatantly attempted to take over the business they had run together. Then resolutely he squelched the bitter thought as he massaged his jaw and watched in growing amusement and wariness Jessica's continued attempts to set up the campground. He knew she couldn't be allowed to stay there for the night, but now he surmised from her earlier actions that it was better to let her come to that conclusion for herself. As he had watched her, though, he had a growing feeling that her stubbornness might prevent that from happening anytime soon.

Throwing him a hateful glance, Jessica turned once

again to the handbook and then produced yet another book or two from the rolled-up sleeping bag. She began in earnest to work on the tent again, and again Clay was reminded that it had been a long time since he had enjoyed the company of a warm woman. As Jessica stretched and pulled, all of her womanly endowments were given full play.

"Having fun?" she called as she stopped for a moment in exhaustion and again wiped rivers of perspiration from her forehead while she scowled at his obviously voyeuristic glances.

"You bet," he answered, completely undaunted. Mischievously he raised his binoculars and focused in on her obvious points of interest.

"How long are you going to stay there?" she demanded while she cringed inwardly as she felt herself coloring again.

"As long as it takes," he answered. A droll smile played over his face as he adjusted the field glasses so he could watch the tiny movements of her face. "This is my property, so I can stay as long as I like."

Turning her back as if to ignore him, she returned to the task at hand. "Well, at least I'll have a decent place to sleep," she said as she tightened the ropes on the tent a final time and gave the instruction book one last glance. "Looks like you could be pretty uncomfortable up there if you're planning to stay long. . . ."

There was an exhilarated touch of confidence in her voice that lasted all of three seconds as something cracked and the tent came fluttering down on one side. "Oh, shhh—" she muttered as she muffled the last letters of the deleted expletive. Resolutely she turned back to the tent and attacked it with a vengeance.

16

"Would you like some help?" he called gently.

"No!" she shouted. "Why don't you just get the hell out of here and leave me alone!"

"Can't do that," he said jovially. "You could be dangerous. God only knows what might happen if you're left alone. . . ."

The grin on his face was maddening and Jessica felt a real impulse to kill. "Go fly a kite," she said vengefully as she reanchored the tent pins and pulled the sides of the tent into place again.

"That sounds like fun," he bantered. He looked up toward the clear blue sky filled with white clouds. "It's a perfect day for it."

"What are you doing up here anyway?" she asked impatiently as she refused the bait of his humor. "Coming around here, carrying a gun . . ."

"I live here," he said as he gestured back toward the way he had come. "And anyone who lives in these woods and mountains should always be prepared to defend himself and his property."

"That sounds paranoid as hell to me," she said derisively. "I mean, I can see you coming to investigate someone trespassing, but the gun is a little much, don't you think?"

"No," he said, suddenly serious. "It's a way of life out here. And to me it's a challenge to try to live in a place where a hard-packed dirt road is the height of civilization."

"Are you serious?" Jessica asked as her frustrations of the moment gave way to a prickling of curiosity that told her reporter's nose that there was something very interesting about all of this.

"I sure am," he said as he arose and came back

down into her campsite. "And now, if you really are intending to stay here, you'd better let somebody show you how."

There was a note of consternation in his voice paradoxically tinged with gentleness, and Jessica found herself responding to it in a rather outrageous way. Her curiosity had instantly mellowed her, but now as he physically neared her again she experienced the full power of his charisma.

He was tall and sexy, virile in a blatantly masculine way, and she felt a strange combination of fascination and attraction that actually embarrassed her for a second or two. But before she could open her mouth to speak he was pulling the tent down.

"Now, just a minute," she protested as she misread his intentions.

"Don't get your dander up," he cautioned as the earlier sparks of humor returned to his eyes. "If you're going to do this, then do it right. First of all, you need to dig a rain trench."

There was something about his presence that seemed to naturally take command and now Jessica found herself following his instructions in an almost unthinking way. For one thing, she was tired of struggling with the tent and she really wanted to know how to pitch it. She listened and watched intently, pulling and tugging when he told her to.

"There," he said, a bit out of breath, twenty minutes later. "That's tight and snug and I doubt that a tornado could carry it off."

"That's great," said Jessica, "and I certainly do appreciate your help, but I think I can manage everything else. . . ."

18

"Now," he said, ignoring her last comment, "if you're going to sleep like a true outdoorsman, you should gather some pine boughs and strip the needles to put beneath your sleeping bag."

"Ugh," she grimaced. "Won't that be prickly?"

"Depends on how you fix your sleeping bag," he said with a sudden suggestive note in his voice. His eyes crinkled appreciatively, highlighting the cleft in his chin again, and Jessica suddenly colored in unexpected demureness as she picked up on the tone of his voice and realized for the first time how very alone she really was.

The protector in Clay was instantly drawn to her in an almost overwhelming way as he noted her shyness and apprehensiveness, and he wondered at his own uncharacteristic boorishness. But then, he also honestly acknowledged how much he was enjoying himself as he looked around to see what else she needed to do.

"You know, I'm serious about your not staying out here alone," he said as he realized that in helping her now she would very probably be encouraged to stay and try to brave this experience out. "Why don't you let me give you a few more pointers, and then when you want to bring your Brownie troop out, I'll help you with them too."

"No way," she said. "And you don't need to help me. I want to do this by myself." The tent standing so beautifully and professionally pitched had given her a false sense of self-confidence, as if she had already forgotten her ineptness and frustrations of a few moments before. "You've taught me the most important thing, and I know I can get the fire pit and food preparation areas set up. We've practiced all of the knots and everything in our meetings."

Clay grimaced as he reached for the manual and saw a diagram of a neatly positioned food area tied and secured between two trees. Bags and pots and all sorts of plastic utensils that Girl Scouts could obviously make in their meetings were featured hanging from trees and spread about. "All right," he said. "This looks pretty good if you can handle it."

"I told you I can handle it," she said as she felt some of her earlier consternation returning. Actually she was beginning to feel a little frustrated by her reactions to this strange man as their minutes together ticked away. It had been a long time since she had experienced this sort of response to another man. Not since the divorce, which had remained essentially friendly between her and Frank, once they had settled their differences. Frank was a very good parent and shared Janey's custody equally with Jessica, allowing Jessica to get the schooling she needed to begin her career as a TV news reporter. Then just as she was really beginning to make progress in her career, Frank was suddenly killed in a car accident and in the last six months Jessica had begun to truly feel the weight of trying to be super single mom, super career woman, super everything, all of which she felt obligated to achieve. This camping trip was the perfect example of that motivation, and the interference of this admittedly attractive, somewhat strange man was leaving her frustrated and confused.

"You're sure about that," said Clay, breaking into her reverie. "Better check the way the wind blows before you start building a fire pit."

As he moved around the area, first glancing at the direction the wind was blowing the trees and then stopping to pick up a pinch of dust and watching it carefully as he released it, Jessica couldn't decide if her fascination with him, which she candidly admitted now, was just natural professional curiosity or something a bit more physical and, therefore, serious. Resolutely she pushed the latter thought away. She didn't have time for such a complication in her life, not even a momentary one, and surely a relationship with a gun-toting fanatic of some sort was anything but desirable.

Then realizing again that she really was very much alone and actually had no idea as to who this man was or what his real intentions were, she decided she had better make a real effort at getting rid of him. "If you don't mind," she said in her most determined voice, "I think you should leave now and let me handle the rest of this myself."

"Well, you're going to be mighty uncomfortable with smoke coming into your tent from the campfire," he answered as he finally ascertained the direction of the wind.

"Did you hear me?" she demanded.

"And what is this?" he asked as he ignored her comments and walked over to the two trees where she had tried to lash two limbs together. He reached down and picked up a long piece of cord.

"Never mind," she said through tight lips as she felt herself growing angry again. "I'm going to fix that right now!" She pulled the nylon cord from his hands and began busily to wrap it around the limbs, which she struggled to support until she could secure them.

21

They slipped, skinning her arm nastily and finally fell down, banging her foot painfully. She could feel tears coming to her eyes and she pulled away as he reached out to help her. "No," she said in a watery voice. "Can't you see that it's important that I'm able to do these things?"

"That's great," he said in frustration as he assured himself that she wasn't badly hurt. "I wish a few more people would take a genuine interest in such things, but wouldn't it make more sense to let someone who knows how show you?"

"How do I know you really know what you're talking about?" she asked heatedly as she brushed the hint of tears away. "You come in here out of nowhere, scaring me to death, spouting off about all of your camping expertise . . ." She gave the last words a derisive emphasis. "I don't even know who you are."

"Well, pardon me," he said in mockery of her emotional outburst. "My name is Clayton Farley and I told you I live about a mile up the way, and"—he added with a lascivious look—"every woman I've ever attacked at gunpoint has lived to tell about it."

"Is that so?" she said as she laughed in response to his rather contrived humor while at the same time she looked at him a little more closely and her reporter's mind took over again. Clayton Farley. There was something about that name that she should know.

"Positive," he answered warmly, apparently unaware of her closer perusal. "And now that you know who I am, how about a reciprocal gesture?"

He extended his hand and Jessica continued to study him and futilely tried to fit the name into her memory. It was a maddening feeling that she couldn't dispel as she finally caught up with herself and hesitantly met his extended hand.

"Jessica," she stammered. "Jessica Andres . . ." In a sudden decidedly covert gesture she deliberately didn't mention her occupation, but as her hand touched his she was immediately impressed with its warmth and smoothness. A warm feeling rushed through her as she looked into his eyes, but at the same time her curious mind observed that such smooth hands were rather strange in an obviously rugged outdoorsman.

"I'm glad to meet you," he said. A little smile played around his eyes again. "And now that we've finished playing silly games, don't you think we'd better get serious about your intention to stay here?" He looked around as if something had just dawned on him. "How in the world did you get all of this stuff in here anyway?" he asked. "Where's your car?"

"I hiked in," she said. "That wasn't too hard to figure out. All of this was in a backpack."

"You are absolutely out of your mind," he said in final incredulity. "How long did that take?"

"I don't know," she said. "What time is it?"

"Does anyone know where you are?" he asked, not waiting for an answer to his previous question as a wave of concern and protectiveness he didn't know he had washed over him.

"Yes, of course," she stammered, realizing she shouldn't reveal that information as again the perilousness of her adventure began to finally dawn on her. Of course she had left word of the area she was going to, but obviously no one would know exactly where she was. Something told her she had nothing to fear

23

from this man, she could trust him, but nevertheless . . .

"So how long did it take you to walk in?" he re-
peated.

"I don't know," she said, "but I'm sure I couldn't
get back to my car before nightfall."

"I'll take you back," he said. "I have a four-wheel
drive."

"No, I really do want to try to do this," she said.
"Can't you understand that I'm not just playing a
game? I didn't realize how remote this area actually is,
but now that I'm here I want to see it through."

The appeal in her voice did something to him. Since
he had moved up here he had dedicated himself to
avoiding relationships that might demand something
from him emotionally, but this was almost like seeing
some defenseless creature that was hurt or in trouble.
He just couldn't abandon her.

"All right, all right," he said. "But if you're going to
insist on doing this to yourself, I'm going to insist that
you let me help you. Otherwise I will bodily pack you
up and get you back to wherever in hell you belong."
A little smile began to creep over his face. "That,
come to think of it, might not be a bad idea anyway,"
he said as he openly scanned her from head to toe.

"I'd fight you to the death," she said in mock melo-
drama as she began to feel the bubbling of uncontrollable laughter in her throat. In sudden release they
both began to laugh together and Jessica felt at that
moment as if they had known each other always but
just now discovered how much they liked each other.

For the next hour they worked untiringly, establishing a neat and tidy campsite. Now the camaraderie

between them seemed perfectly natural. "There," said Clay as he looked around in satisfaction. "All you need now is firewood and pine needles. C'mon. I'll show you how to do that too."

In perfect accord Jessica followed him, doing as he instructed. Once she settled down and swallowed her pride, she was fascinated and honestly pleased to be learning so much. And with every moment she grew more confident that she would be able to create a wonderful camping experience for Janey and the other Brownies, which made her feel very good. But she also found her eyes trailing after Clay. He was definitely an enigma. She was completely fascinated, and her reporter's instincts told her there was a story here. All she had to do was find it.

"Over this way," he called as they gathered armloads of wood.

"But that's on *your* property," she said with theatrical emphasis.

He turned and gave her a wide grin. "I think I can trust you this far," he said.

She laughed again and realized it had been a long time since she had laughed so much in one day. And as his last words rang about her something about them pleased her exceedingly. She had the feeling that there was a sincere compliment included in that banter.

The ambience of the outdoors finally began to truly affect Jessica as she breathed in the cool pine air and reveled in the warm rays of the setting sun. She dropped another load of firewood in the campsite and went back following Clay's lead as he began to cut and gather pine boughs. She had a marvelous sense of purpose as she went about these tasks, as well as, she finally acknowledged, security when she was in Clay's presence. Now she truly realized what a folly this whole undertaking would have been, and she was overwhelmed with joy as she realized that thanks to him she was going to pull it off.

She was deep in thought, not really watching where she was going, when suddenly she found herself on a precipice that dropped sheer hundreds of feet. She gasped as her breath quickened and she felt herself tighten in an uncontrollable paralysis. She tried to speak and couldn't open her mouth, let alone utter a sound. She felt herself giving into vertigo and realized in just a few seconds she could tumble over that ledge with no way of saving herself. She closed her eyes, feeling completely helpless as waves of panic washed over her. Her face was ashen as she clutched the knife and pine boughs to her body.

"Cl . . . Cl . . . Clay . . ." she finally uttered as the whole world began to spin around her. Her voice was barely a whisper, but Clay had already grown alarmed when he remembered the cliff that was there at the edge of the trees.

"I'm here," he shouted as he came upon her. "Just don't move. Whatever you do, don't move!"

The tone of his voice and the command it imparted somehow brought her to for just a moment, but as the sweep of the distant panorama below came into her vision again, Jessica knew she had never been so frightened in her life.

"Jessica," said Clay in a soft voice now, "I'm coming for you. You don't have to do a thing. Just wait for me." Slowly he moved toward her, reaching his arms out to her. "Look at me, Jessica. Don't look anywhere else. Come to me. . . ."

"I . . . I . . . can't," she cried in a tiny voice. "I can't. . . ."

"Yes, you can," he said as he reached her and grabbed her, pulling her close in his embrace.

She melted into his arms and buried her face in his shoulder as her body sagged in relief. "I've never been so scared," she said as tears began to fall.

"It's all right," he soothed her as he moved her away from the edge of the cliff, still safely ensconced in his arms. "Apparently you're afraid of heights. Has this ever happened to you before?"

"No, I don't think so," she said as she began to resume her earlier demeanor. "But that place is so high that it would scare anyone to death. You should put something there, a railing or something. . . ."

"No one is ever here except me," he said firmly. He squared his jaw in determination again. "I don't want strangers tramping around here, and that's one of the things that keeps them out."

She gave him a startled look as she began to squirm from his embrace. "Don't you think you carry this recluse mania or whatever it is of yours a little too far?"

A strange look came over his face as his arm tightened and pulled her firmly into his embrace again. Tenderness punctuated by a little smile washed over his features. "You may be right," he said in a low, husky voice. "I wouldn't have been very happy if something had happened to you over there."

Clay gestured with his head toward the cliff and sparks began to invade his eyes as Jessica marveled at

27

his chameleonlike personality. Both of them began to react to the physical intimacy of the embrace and suddenly Jessica felt a longing such as she had never experienced before. In perfect mesmerized communion he reached down and touched her lips with his own. It was a fleeting and sweet caress that ignited into something powerful and demanding as he pulled her closer and kissed her with a deep probing masterfulness that left them both weak and disoriented. Jessica felt herself melting as she clung to him. In perfect accord he began slowly to drop with her to the ground as he savored her skin and eyes and lips in a ritual of tenderness as old as time. In a moment of ecstasy and dreamy unconsciousness of the reality of the situation Jessica responded with a fire and need she didn't know existed before that moment.

"Jessie," he breathed as his lips sought out hers again and again, "I had no idea there could be such magic in this world."

She sensed the beginning of a stronger, more demanding insistence on his part and suddenly began to realize as the boughs beneath her head prickled her neck that this was indeed a real experience and it shouldn't be happening. At least not with a perfect stranger that she had just met that afternoon in rather uncertain circumstances to say the least, and certainly not here in the grass and dirt of a remote area far from anyone she knew or trusted.

"Stop," she said abruptly as his lips again left her feeling weak and she wondered anew what had allowed her to put herself in such a precarious position.

"Why?" he asked as he looked into her eyes and continued to caress her with his hands. The tingling aromatic forest breeze ruffled his hair, accenting the electric-blue of his eyes, and Jessica knew she had never been with anyone more desirable or attractive in her life. For that reason alone she couldn't allow this to happen in this way.

"Because I'm asking you to," she said as she pulled away from him. "For all of the obvious reasons . . ." She met his eyes in a direct challenge and covered her breasts in a protective gesture. "I wouldn't want the warm moments we've just shared ruined by something we both know isn't right."

He knew at that moment that he could force her and have his way with her right there. She wasn't that unwilling, and she knew it too. But she never wavered in her appeal as something told her that this was a challenge she had to win. Not just for the moment, but for the future as well—at the same time everything within her was shrieking for the wanting of him and she knew the memory of this man and this moment would haunt her for the rest of her life.

"You're right, of course," he said as he visibly regained control of himself and answered the appeal in her eyes. "I'm sorry. It was just an irresistible moment." He arose and reached out to help her to her feet. His eyes met hers and they both searched for understanding as the intimacy of their touch sparked a tenderness neither could deny.

"I understand," she said. "And I'm truly grateful for the way you helped me back there. . . ." Her voice trailed off as she tried to think of something inane or trite that would render the whole scene meaningless, but she failed miserably.

He watched her with mixed emotions of need and

anxiety. Something about her made him worry, which was more than a little perplexing, but worse than that, he suddenly realized for the first time how lonely his chosen existence really was. And this woman with her crazy stubbornness and spirit all rolled up with endearing vulnerabilities was someone he didn't want to lose.

"Let me get you back to the campground," he said. "I'll help you get your campfire and supper started and make sure you're going to be all right for the night."

"Really, you've done enough," she said as she brushed off her clothes and retrieved the pine boughs.

"That's not the agreement we made," he said as he took her arm and began helping her down the slope to the camp area. There was a strength and firmness all about him, and Jessica knew it was useless to argue. Suddenly she was glad that that was the way it was.

Clay spoke very little as the campfire began to dance merrily. He matter-of-factly pointed out the essentials of the things she should know and both of them began to feel the strain as the emotions and desires of those few fiery moments continued to fill the atmosphere. He looked at her often with a hungry quizzical expression and she looked away, fearful that she might do something to encourage him. Finally, as Jessica pushed warmed-up beans and bread around on her plate and the campfire was the only light in the darkness, he got up and threw his coffee into the fire all in one swift movement. "I'm going to check and see that you have enough pine needles beneath your sleeping bag, and I guess it's probably time to call it a night."

"You're going away?" Her voice was a bit apprehensive as the gloom of darkness finally penetrated her consciousness.

"You never intended for me to stay the night, did you?" There was a hint of a mischievous smile on his face. It crinkled his eyes in a fascinating way and filled her with warmth.

"No . . . no," she answered as she responded with a little smile of her own and was inwardly pleased to see that aspect of him again.

"Well, when you're a veteran camper you'll probably find that it's best to follow nature's clock. Go to bed when the sun sets and get up when it rises."

"I think you're right," she said as a little yawn escaped from her. "I can honestly say I'm beat."

"Okay, then. Sleep tight. I'll stop by to see you in the morning, but if you need anything, just call my name. I'm not that far away."

"Will do," she said as she savored the look on his face through the campfire and tried to stifle the hint of a shiver that ran down her spine when she realized she was going to be alone in the dark.

"Take care of your campfire the way I told you to," he said as he reached for his rifle. Her face was a caricature of a wide-eyed orphan child as she stared at him through the flames. He swallowed and took a deep breath. "I'll stay if you want me to," he said.

"No, no," she stammered. "I'll be all right. . . ."

"It's no problem," he said. "I'd be glad to do it."

"No, really," she said as some of her earlier spirit revived. "You'd freeze to death and there's only one sleeping bag." Their eyes simultaneously traveled to the tent and focused on the neatly made sleeping area that rested on a deep bed of pine needles. Their

31

thoughts were identical and they both knew it as Jessica felt herself redden with longing and a warm liquid feeling rushed through her. "I know I can manage," she said weakly.

He looked at her for a long moment and understood completely how impossible it would be for them to stay apart should they continue to be so close in the small circle of firelight, the dark woods, and glittering night sky. The chemistry was there, instantaneous and ready to ignite, and if he so much as took one step toward her, he doubted that either one of them would be able to stop. He gave her one last glance as he began to move slowly away. He turned after a few steps, gave her a little wave, and then walked slowly toward his snug cabin.

An hour later he was pacing the floor restlessly. Finally he smashed his fist into his hand and went to gather his outdoor gear. A few moments later he was securely positioned above Jessica's quiet camp. He noted with satisfaction that she had banked the campfire correctly and he could see her safely ensconced in the sleeping bag through the last flickering embers of the fire. He leaned his gun against a nearby tree and rolled out his bedroll, leaving the flashlight near the top. Still restless, he couldn't relax, and as Jessica finally gave in to slumber, the shadow over her tent was of a lonely caring man standing against the night sky.

CHAPTER TWO

The next morning when Jessica arose she grimaced in pain. Every inch of her was stiff and sore and she was sure that rocks had replaced the pine needles beneath her bedroll. "Ohh," she moaned as she crawled awkwardly from the tent. Everything was hazy and damp and she shivered in the early morning cold. What she wanted more than anything else was a scalding cup of coffee and a warm fire or, better yet, her own bed and warm, snug house. "Deliver me," she petitioned as she ran her hands through her tangled hair and yearned for the refreshing taste of toothpaste and the privacy of her own bathroom.

Although she had fashioned an area for that purpose, a blanket enclosure behind a bush left a lot to be desired. She scrubbed her face and tried to calm her nearly uncontrollable shivers as she shakily piled kindling into the fire pit. She struck a match and her eyes watered as a suffocating plume of smoke began to drift into her face. The bright, sparkling outdoorsy feeling that had characterized this place yesterday afternoon was cold and almost sinister now as a chilling mist moved in and left everything soaked. Furiously Jessica tried again and again to get the fire started, but it was no use. "Why?" she asked as she looked around. Why couldn't just one thing work the first time around?

"Having trouble?" asked a familiar voice as Clay came toward her through the mist.

"I guess you could say that," she said resignedly. All the fight and spirit of the day before were gone. She was cold and tired and sore, and she had honestly had enough of this. She looked at him expectantly.

He looked into her weary eyes and felt those strong protective feelings again but was somewhat saddened by this degeneration of her spirit. "I think anyone who tried to start a fire on a morning like this would have trouble," he said reassuringly as his eyes dwelled on the small pitiful spiral of smoke rising from the damp wood.

"You wouldn't say that just to make me feel better, would you?" she asked as a tiny vestige of her former independence emerged.

"Are you kidding?" he replied. "It's practically raining right now. Why don't you get your things together and come on up to my cabin for coffee and breakfast?"

"Do you have a bathroom?" she asked as his proposal was more than a little enticing.

"All of the comforts of home," he said as he reached down to give her a hand up from her stooped position. A big grin lit up his face as he noted her discomfiture over her appearance. "Outdoor life and glamor just don't seem to mix, do they?"

34

"Forget about glamor," she said derisively. "Just the basic creature comforts are all I'm interested in right now." A big laugh bellowed from him as she gave the sleeping bag a little kick and quickly gathered her basic needs into a small bag which she slung over her shoulder. "I'm all yours," she said impishly. "And to think I sold out for a bathroom."

"When you get down to the bottom line," he said, smiling jovially and again illuminating his rugged features in an appealing way, "you soon learn that the basics are always a top priority."

"So I'm definitely learning," she said mockingly as she pulled her jacket around her body a little more snugly.

"C'mon," he said with a grin as he placed his arm around her in comradely fashion. "I think you've learned enough for one day."

She nestled against his rugged clothes and was glad to be heading for civilization. Everything about their conversation seemed to be natural and relaxed, and Jessica was far too uncomfortable to think rationally about Clay's early appearance or the easy intimacy they were enjoying now. As they reached the grassy knoll where he had watched over her, he stooped to grab his neatly rolled sleeping bag and pointed the way up the path.

Taking all of this in, Jessica looked at him strangely. "You stayed out here last night?" she said incredulously as she immediately perceived exactly what had happened and felt almost flabbergasted. Something told her this was a man who truly respected her, yet one who would always protect her and in spite of all the modern notions of female independence the feeling struck something deep and primitive within her which left her feeling wonderful. She gave him her biggest smile and reached for his hand. "Thanks," she said. "I really mean that."

Their eyes locked and Clay again felt distinctly uncomfortable as he also battled and wondered at his rather unnatural actions. "I couldn't leave you out here alone," he said rather off-handedly. "Might have had a bear or something come snooping around . . ."

"Bear?" she said, a bit alarmed. Then she laughed. "Oh, you're putting me on," she said as she saw his eyes crinkling.

"No, I'm not," he said. "See those berry bushes all over the place?"

Jessica looked around carefully and for the first time noticed untidy bushes that seemed to be dotted with red.

"Sure sign of bear," he said as he drolly anticipated her reaction.

"Now you tell me," she said in real outrage.

"Well, if you recall, you thought you knew it all yesterday. You probably wouldn't have believed me."

"That's not true," she said as a little huffiness entered her voice and he smiled. "Seems to me like I listened to you more than once."

He looked at her and they were both suddenly transported into another time as they remembered simultaneously those few soul-shattering moments when they had clung to each other after he had rescued her from the cliff.

"Didn't I . . . ?" she asked self-consciously as her face colored and she looked to the ground. Then she took a deep breath and looked him square in the eye.

36

He saw a depth of emotion and turmoil that matched his own. "I want you to know how deeply I appreciate your concern and your respect for me. I won't ever forget it."

"I hope not," he said softly. The currents were traveling between them again, gathering strength, and both of them knew it would take only seconds to again reach the fiery intensity of those aching caresses from the evening before. He reached out and awkwardly touched her cheek as he juggled his burdens. "I sincerely hope not."

Jessica smiled, not knowing what to say, and felt her heart begin to race. She knew this was something she had never experienced before. There was a depth to her rapport with this man that was impossible and beautiful at the same time. Common sense told her everything about it was irrational, aside from the fact that this was a man whom she had just happened upon yesterday, and whom, for all intents and purposes, she knew absolutely nothing about.

But again her professional curiosity prickled as something about the name Clayton Farley continued to aggravate her. Maybe she knew more than she realized, but now, as she looked into his eyes and gave him her hand to help her up a steep place in the hill, she was determined to find out for both personal and professional reasons.

"Is it far?" she asked after they had walked wordlessly for several moments. Her words were coming out in little pants as she struggled to get her breath.

"No," he said as they walked into a clearing. He waved his arm expansively and there, several hundred yards away in a sun-bathed clearing, was a compact cabin straight out of a storybook. "I call it Owl Hill," he said as he watched her expression.

Jessica immediately noted the telescope on the porch and remembered the field glasses from the day before. He obviously did mean every word he said about strangers on his land. In sudden perception she wondered what or whom he was hiding from. Then she noticed that the area surrounding the cabin was carefully organized in obviously productive garden plots, and as they neared the front steps she saw a cow and chickens farther back next to a barn that matched the cabin. Bees swarmed from a hive and went busily about their tasks in a nearby orchard.

"This is something," she said in real admiration as she sublimated her earlier curious thoughts. "You must be very proud of it."

"Yes, I am," he said a tad sheepishly as he massaged the back of his head nervously. He helped her up the steps to the porch, carefully unlocked a big, heavy door, and pushed through a large inner screen door. "If I had to," he continued, "I think I could live here for years and never need a thing from the outside world."

"By yourself?" asked Jessica as it suddenly dawned on her that she hadn't even asked him about his family or work or anything. Somehow she had just fallen into this trusting limbo, and now for the second time since yesterday she suddenly realized she might very well be doing a most foolhardy thing as she followed this strange man into his home.

"By myself," he said.

"Are you really serious?" asked Jessica as her eyes

widened. "Are you saying you've never allowed any-one else to see this?"

He turned and gave her a strange look. "Well, basically, yeah. I guess you could say that." He seemed to be a little uncomfortable, as if the fact that she was actually there had just dawned on him.

"Isn't that pretty lonely?" she asked again. "I mean, if you live here all of the time . . ." Her reporter's nose was in full play as the word *exclusive* began to play around her brain teasingly.

"Yes and no," he said rather off-handedly. "Whenever I want to, I spend time in town. I just don't make a big deal out of this place to anyone."

"But I'd think you'd want to show it off," exclaimed Jessica as she moved around the comfortable room and pictured how she might add a touch of color here and there, but for the most part she loved it just the way it was.

"Not really," he responded as he gave her a bit of an exasperated glance. "Look. The bathroom's that way," he said as he pointed down a long hallway that was lined with shellacked cedar paneling. "You go do what you have to do and I'll see about some breakfast for us."

A little grin played over his face as he took her by her shoulders and sent her on her way. But as Jessica moved in the direction he had indicated, she had the distinct feeling that she had just been subtly told to mind her own business. Suddenly the challenge of the situation excited her in an exhilarating way. The atmosphere of mystery and security that emanated from this place definitely appealed to her reporter's instinct.

She could see, at the very minimum, a fantastic human interest story coming out of this.

The bathroom was roomy and Jessica quickly located large soft towels and other necessary toiletries. With a sigh she turned on the hot water and reveled in its feel on her face as she lathered and washed her complexion to a shining cleanness. One look at her hair and the rest of her body told her that wasn't going to do it. Without thinking she dropped her clothes and turned on the spigots in the bathtub. A few moments later she was leaning back in the steaming tub, breathing in the wood scent of the house, and luxuriating in the feel of the soap on her body. Taking a bath had never in her entire life seemed so enjoyable as this.

"Hey, how long are you going to stay in there?" asked Clay as he gave a sharp rap to the door and startled Jessica from her reverie.

"I'm taking a bath," she called. "I couldn't resist it. . . ."

"Some outdoor woman," he said derisively.

But Jessica knew he was smiling, and somehow the thought of him outside that door waiting for her to come out was more than a little sensuous and she found herself liking that idea very much. "I'll be out in a moment," she called. Then as she allowed herself to deliciously dwell on that frankly titillating thought she began to smell bacon and eggs and she suddenly understood anew what Clay was talking about when he mentioned basic motivations and needs. Hunger had to be number one, but she also had a feeling that these other churnings and waves within her body could not be far behind.

She quickly shampooed her hair and toweled herself

dry with brisk movements. There was a hint of curl in her shoulder-length tresses and she expertly flicked them into a tousled style that left her looking like an inviting gamin. She quickly put on fresh underwear, which she retrieved from her knapsack, and glanced around for her other clothes. She took one look at that rumpled heap on the floor and turned her nose up derisively.

"Clay," she called as she carefully wrapped a towel around her body. "Would you have a spare shirt until I can get back down to the camp for a change of clothes?"

"Good grief," he said as she poked her head around the bathroom door and met his laughing eyes. "I only ask you up for breakfast. The next thing I know you'll be moving in."

"You wish," she said as she emerged and suddenly dared him to make something out of this. "Look, just find me an old shirt that I can put on over my jeans. I just can't handle putting that shirt on again."

Clay sucked in his breath and looked at her, his eyes traveling from her head to her toes as she moved toward him. "Lady, do you know what you're doing to me?" he asked.

"Causing you to burn the bacon," she said in sudden alarm as dark smoke began to swirl down the hall.

"Damn it to hell," he shouted as he raced to the kitchen.

Jessica followed him and grimaced when he grabbed the hot handle of the cast-iron skillet and yelled out in pain. "Oh, no," she cried as she used the edge of her towel to move the pan away from the fire.

"This wouldn't have happened at all if . . ." His

words trailed off. His eyes were fierce when they met hers and in sudden uncontrollable frustration he reached out and drew her close, devouring her mouth with deep kisses that seemed to set the rest of their bodies on fire.

Time stopped between them as they both felt the pull of a destiny they knew they couldn't deny. Jessica felt her hands loosening on the towel and the invitation of the bed in the other room was like a magnet drawing them together.

"I want you. My God, I want you," he breathed as his lips traveled down her neck. "But it won't work. . . . I know it won't."

He pulled away abruptly and Jessica found herself reaching for his back. "Clay, it's all right," she said, still shaken herself from their explosive encounter. "Let me see how badly you're burned," she managed to ask in a calm tone.

Slowly he turned around and looked deeply into her eyes. He held his hand out which was red, but not blistered. Then he opened his arms and pulled her into a soft embrace. "This is crazy, I know it is," he said as he tousled her damp hair. He nuzzled her skin and openly savored the perfume of her newly washed body as he ran his uninjured hand over the towel and searched out the curves beneath it. Jessica felt herself responding in a wild and abandoned way, and yet there was a curious restraint too. He lifted her chin and searched her eyes as she wordlessly met his lips in a soft kiss that melded them together in a sweet, trusting ecstasy. Then they pulled away, allowing only their fingertips to touch as they silently communed, and both tried to fathom the real meaning of this en-

42

counter. "Should we talk about this"—they laughed as the words tumbled from both of them simultaneously —"over breakfast?" Clay turned her toward the bedroom with a playful swat. "Go on. Find yourself a shirt and I'll fry some more bacon and try not to burn it or myself up."

Jessica gave him a happy smile and returned a few moments later dressed in one of his shirts, which gave her a floppy, comfortable look. From that moment on it was as if they had known each other for a thousand years and they'd sat together for breakfast like this every morning. Haltingly, as she drank steaming coffee and ate bacon and eggs, Jessica told him about Frank and her marriage and the way she worried about Janey and sometimes felt guilty—especially when she thought of beginning a relationship with another man.

"Guilty? What do you have to feel guilty about?" he asked as he stopped his fork in mid-motion and honestly questioned her.

"I don't know," she said a little sheepishly. "It's just that in a way I never left Frank. . . ."

"You were divorced, weren't you?"

"Yes, but we were still close."

"Then you still loved him?"

"No," she said, shaking her head as she thought now of her raging feelings for the man sitting across from her. "It was just that we had Janey to think about and we seemed to get along better after the divorce. It was comfortable. There were no ties or power struggles."

Clay looked at her carefully as he neatly folded his napkin and laid it aside. He felt a real need to completely understand her. "Sounds to me like you were putting it together again. I think you're more of a widow than a divorcée."

Jessica looked at him as if he were opening doors in her mind. She could feel herself beginning to understand the turmoil and anxiety as well as the anger and loneliness she had experienced since Frank's death.

"So, you're responding to your grief," he went on, "by trying to be Supermom. That's obvious. Otherwise why would you ever have . . ." His voice trailed off, as if he were trying to understand her actions. "I think it's an insidious sort of guilt trip that has you literally trying to be three or four people at one time. You're probably attempting things that you would normally be more sensible about."

"Oh, brother," said Jessica, laughing as she met his intense eyes and reddened. "I guess that makes us both a couple of Looney Toons, doesn't it? Here you are, obviously hiding from the world, and I'm trying to whip it in one day!"

A little smile began to play over his face as he realized his amateur analysis had struck home, tuning in perfectly to her vibes. And, too, he was intrigued with her adroit use of humor to sidestep the issue. "Sounds like a perfect match to me," he said as he arose and moved around to massage her shoulders playfully. "I hope the way we're getting along means we'll be seeing each other again."

"You're sure I wouldn't end up getting shot or something? I mean, considering your aversion to strangers and all . . ." She looked up at him coyly and felt the warmth of his hands radiating to her toes as her blood began to pound again.

44

"I'll guarantee it," he said huskily.

Their eyes locked and both seemed suddenly to be searching for words.

"Well, then, let's just leave it at that," said Jessica. "When you're in town give me a call."

"Oh, I have a phone here," he said as he pointed to a mass of electronics equipment in the corner. "I probably have the most sophisticated private communication system in the area."

"All right," she said laughing. "I'm in the book."

"I'll find you," he said confidently, "but in the meantime let's go down and get you packed up. I'm going to drive you back to your car."

"B-but," she sputtered.

"No buts," he said authoritatively. "Just remember there is such a thing as being too independent for your own good."

"Out of the horse's mouth," she said jokingly as they both burst into laughter.

"You should know," he said as he gave her a wry look. "Now, why don't you help me clean off the table and then I'll show you around before we leave."

"I'd like that," she said as she looked at him for a long moment and again felt a real sense of comfort and acceptance. It was just perfect to feel so good about something. "The whole place looks fascinating."

He grinned in obvious delight. "C'mon," he said as they placed the last of the dishes in the sink.

For the next hour they wandered over the meticulously planned area. Jessica saw the generators powered by both wind and solar power, and as they walked from neatly planted plot after plot their fingers seemed to surreptitiously come together until they were walking hand in hand. The animals in the barn fascinated her and she laughed outrageously when Clay gave her a lesson in milking a cow. Again she marveled at how smooth his hands were and wondered how he kept them that way. She soon learned how as he reached for a pitchfork to throw some hay into the cow's stall and grabbed a worn pair of gloves at the same time. Her reporter's radar immediately tuned into this and again her professional curiosity signaled to her.

In the house he helped her down into his root cellar and the feel of his strong grip on her waist as he steadied her down the ladder was more than a little heady and stimulating. The look in his eyes as he turned her around and brushed her lips lightly with his own told her his reaction was the same, but by some unspoken mutual pact they both seemed to restrain themselves, as though they were telling themselves that they were two sensible adults who knew it was too soon to be acting this way, but the time would come. The currents between them were too intense, though, to avoid the little gestures of endearment that continued to happen almost unconsciously.

Jessica was impressed with his vast storage areas and his stores of staples consisting mainly of whole grains, legumes, dried milk, and honey. "You seem to be ready for anything," she said.

"I think I am," he answered. "That's what's been so fascinating about all of this. When I decided to come out here and live I had this obsession with the idea of living an existence something like a caveman utilizing modern technologies. It was important that I understand, and build, and experience everything myself."

"It looks like you've done it too," said Jessica.

"Yes," he said. "But most of all I wanted to be in a position where I would never again have to rely on another person. Now that I've done it, I can't tell you what it means to be self-sufficient in such a primitive way. It's brought me great peace, and I'm very protective of it."

"I can understand that," said Jessica. "But honestly, aren't you lonely?" she asked as a touch of real concern entered her voice. "Out here all by yourself?"

"Not really," he replied. Their eyes locked and he flinched under her probing. "At least I don't think I've ever noticed it much until yesterday. . . ."

"And what happened yesterday?" she asked coyly.

"Oh, nothing of real importance," he said as a mischievous grin began to play over his face, "except I met this beautiful wacky woman who is living proof that I'm not as wacky as she thinks I am."

"I did all right," she said as she felt a little honest outrage. "I made it through the night."

"One day without a bath and perfumed soap," he said with an exaggerated pucker on his lips while he continued to grin at her. "Probably for you that was pretty good."

"You take that back," she said as she tried to grab his arm. "Every bone in my body is shrieking from sleeping on the ground."

"My point exactly," he said. "You need to either harden yourself up by staying outside for several months a little at a time or else plan better for the continued comforts of home when you go on these outings."

"And you're the one who could teach me all of

that," she said as she laughed and began to warm from his touch.

"That I can," he said as he pulled her into a playful embrace. "But you know there are comforts and then there are comforts. You may have to take some things out in trade."

"Oh," she said as she felt a core of fire spin through her stomach. "What did you have in mind?"

"Whatever I can get," he said as he pulled her closer. "I'm beginning to understand why nature usually requires a minimum of two of anything if it is to survive."

"Sounds like it could be interesting," she said as she lifted her lips to his and was immediately drowning in the passion of the embrace as the fire within their bodies suddenly roared and demanded satisfaction. Weakly she pulled away, knowing she could no longer resist him. In a flash he pulled her back to him and probed her mouth with his parrying tongue while his hands played over her back and began to push the folds of the oversize shirt away. He groaned and nibbled the skin on her neck as he reached down to cup her breast.

"Let's go up to the bed," he said. "I can't stand this anymore."

"No," she said weakly, "I don't think that's the thing to do. . . ." Her voice trailed off as he scoured her ear with his tongue and her body was wracked with chills that made her grab and cling to him. He picked her up and began moving toward the ladder.

"Go on," he said as his eyes glazed with passion and his breathing grew erratic. "Otherwise it's going to happen right here."

48

In a haze Jessica climbed the ladder with Clay right behind her, his hands steadying her waist and driving her crazy. He pushed her through the trap door and then pulled her to him as he stretched her body next to his on the floor. In deliberate feasting motions filled with sounds of rapture he cherished every inch of her exposed skin. His lips moved over her nipples as he pushed her bra away and succored them into inviting peaks. She buried her hands in his hair and arched her body in ecstasy as she responded with an ardor she had never experienced before. He moved over her and suddenly the weight of his strong body was too much for her sore muscles and joints.

"Oh," she cried as she grimaced. "Not here, Clay. This floor is too hard."

Instantly he was overwhelmed with guilt when he saw the pain in her face. "I'm sorry," he said, genuinely contrite, and both of them knew the moment was over. Honestly chagrined, they helped each other up and quickly dusted their clothes off, seeking a diversion in that activity. "I'm beginning to think we have a problem," he said. "I've never . . ."

"I know," she said. "That makes two of us."

"Well," he said in obvious frustration. "What are we going to do about it?" She saw him glance toward the bedroom furtively.

"Give ourselves time," she said softly. "That's really the whole problem. I have a feeling we're both fairly old-fashioned and conventional about these things."

He nodded and a small smile played over his face. "I guess you're right," he said. "And I know we don't know each other well enough, but, lady, you sure turn me inside out, and time isn't going to matter much longer."

She met his eyes in mutual agreement. "Then I think I'd better go," she said. "Let's wait and see how we feel about this in a week or so."

"You're on," he said as he gave her chin a little nudge. Their eyes met and again they both felt a time-immemorial kinship that made them perfectly comfortable with each other.

A few moments later Clay took her back to her camp in his four-wheel drive and then drove her and her belongings back to her car. As they finished transferring her backpack to her vehicle, Clay looked at her again for a long moment. The silence stretched between them and Jessica felt herself beginning to grow uneasy as she, also, searched for appropriate words. She longed to reach out and touch him, but now that she was actually leaving him she was curiously shy. Swallowing, she listened as words began to tumble through her lips. "You really have a fascinating place, Clay. I'd love to show it to Janey and our Brownie troop."

"We might work that out," he said after another long moment in which he probed her eyes and seemed to examine her soul again. "But you also know how I feel about strangers."

"Clay," she said as she felt a hint of impatience, "don't you think it would be better to share the knowledge you've gained here rather than to chase people away?"

"Spoken like a true idealist," he said fondly as his grin returned and he reached out to touch her cheek.

"You could think about it," she said as she climbed into her car.

"Maybe," he said as he reached in to caress her face again. "I guess it's a thought." She met his eyes and smiled. He leaned in to give her another soft kiss. "Until next time, then?"

"Until next time," she replied as she started her car with a roar.

It wasn't until she was far down the road that Jessica began to puzzle over some of Clay's last words and she realized that she had learned very little about him. She knew no hard, factual things—where he came from, what he did for a living. All of that talk and intimacy and her reporter's mind hadn't ferreted out a single significant solid fact about him other than that he was obviously a recluse with some rather philosophical goals implemented in a very practical situation, and he obviously knew how to garden and take care of animals and still have smooth hands.

In chagrin she realized her personal needs had far outweighed her professional curiosity, but as a sweet warmth replaced that feeling she wasn't in any way disappointed. Still her curiosity needled her. There was a story there and Clay shouldn't be afraid to share it. Now she owed it to herself and him in more ways than one to find it.

CHAPTER THREE

"So who cares," shouted a gruff Jim Reynolds, the news director at KROY-TV and Jessica's boss. "So a guy is living in a cabin like a hermit or something. Do you call that news?"

"His name is Clayton Farley," Jessica insisted, "and I just know it would make a great human interest story.

"It doesn't sound like he's too eager to do something like that," fumed Jim. "Haven't you ever heard of invasion of privacy?"

"But if I can talk him into it?"

"Forget it," said Jim in finality. "Now get your buns over to City Hall and cover the story I assigned to you."

Jessica left him with a sigh and went out to meet her partner and cameraman for that day. "No go?" said Kevin Myers when he saw her face.

"You've got it," she said dejectedly.

"I wouldn't wonder," said Kevin. "I just heard that

Farley is a big advertising executive. He probably does business with the station and they wouldn't touch that with a ten-foot pole."

"You're kidding," said Jessica. Suddenly she felt very angry. She knew this was a good story and she was going to cover it whether they wanted it or not.

That night she paced the floor after she had put Janey to bed. She had tried to find Clay's telephone number, only to learn that it was unlisted. She had hoped she would hear from him by now, but it had been only a few days since her ill-fated excursion. Kevin's disclosures about Clay had definitely been unsettling, and it took only Jessica's very basic skills as a reporter to learn that Clay was the president of Acme Associates, one of the biggest advertising agencies in the area and that for the past few years he had more or less run the place through remote control. He was in town only occasionally, but still supervised and exercised the final control over all of the company projects after meeting once or twice with a client. The rest he neatly delegated to trusted people whom he paid well, thus creating a mystery too tantalizing for Jessica to ignore. *That explains the smooth hands,* thought Jessica. *He obviously is a corporate dropout and he really doesn't want anyone to know what he is up to.*

But then, she asked herself, what reason could he have for withdrawing from society in such an extreme way? She could understand what he said about challenges and basics, but he was being deliberately reclusive, and, yes, selfish, Jessica insisted to herself. And yet she knew he was a gentle and kind person who must obviously get along with people in order to be such a successful businessman. Open and sunny by nature, Jessica simply couldn't imagine why anyone would want to live such an obviously lonely and sheltered existence.

If only I could spend some time with him, I know I could get him to open up, she thought as warm waves of remembrance washed over her and she definitely knew she wanted to see this man for much more than just a story. Not one day or night had gone by without her remembering the touch of his hands or the warmth of his caresses. She wasn't sorry for their restraint because she felt there could be only good things in their future, but she was beginning to grow anxious over his lack of a call.

Finally she had resolutely decided to try and get in touch with him herself only to run into the dead end of the unlisted number. She could just picture him allowing his distrust of strangers to interfere with his honest desires and she firmly decided she just couldn't let that happen. She had the Brownie troop story to use as her excuse and she decided then and there to pay him a visit the next day.

The next morning her little car labored over rugged roads until at last she saw the trail leading to Clay's clearing. Jessica was almost certain he was following her progress through his telescope or binoculars by now, and she hoped fervently that he remembered what her car looked like, although she still had trouble believing he would actually shoot at someone. She glanced back and furtively looked at the small video camera and tape deck that was part of her personal home video recording equipment and pursed her lips in firm resolution.

54

As Clay watched her car coming up the rutted road, he swore. "Damn it," he said.

After Jessica had left him it took only a few days before he had known he was in serious trouble. Never had a woman affected him in such a manner. He wanted her desperately, but it took only a few hours alone for his more rational side to remind him how impossible such a relationship would be.

Then he had grown angry as he remembered again how he had trusted his former partner, Clare. It was his special management genius that had created a corporate structure that practically ran itself just as his current situation did. But in the past he had spent his time traveling and in general having a good time, especially with the ladies. Then in one fell swoop of unadulterated greed Clare had nearly destroyed both him and their company. The attendant infighting and corporate struggles that had followed had left him permanently soured.

It wasn't any small consideration that she had been a woman and he in his trusting naiveté had failed to attribute the possibility of such tactics to her for that reason. Ultimately he had bought her out and reestablished his earlier business success while also gravitating to the solace of his present life.

As he considered it rationally he frankly questioned his instinctive trust of Jessica, who was also a woman, but even more objectively he knew Jessica could realistically never live like this, far away from people. And he was so firmly entrenched in it and the peace it gave him that he knew he didn't want to change either. Utilizing his strongest self-control, he had finally promised himself he simply wouldn't call Jessica or see her again. Now here she was coming in here as if she already owned the place. Despite his resolve to remain unmoved, he knew from the moment he set eyes on her he was in deep trouble all over again.

He had tried to rationalize the whole scene of the other day, telling himself that he had simply denied himself a woman for too long, but as Jessica stepped from the car all breathy with excitement and a happy smile, her hair swinging so saucily over her shoulders, he could have killed her for making him want her so much.

"Hi, Clay," she said a little too enthusiastically. "I hope you don't mind. . . . I know you said you'd call me, but when I told Janey and the other Brownies about your place they were crazy to see it. I realized when I got home that I could never get all of them up here, so I brought my video recorder camera and I thought I might show it to them on tape next week."

"Tape?" he asked, obviously a bit confused by her rapid chatter, only a bit of which he was listening to.

"Videotape," said Jessica. "You know. The kind you use in a home video recorder."

"I don't know about that," he said a bit testily.

"Well, you don't have to be in it," said Jessica rapidly. "For goodness' sake, it's only for a little Brownie troop. All I want is a few shots of the gardens and animals. Maybe the storage areas . . ."

"Oh, all right," he said in exasperation.

Jessica looked at him sharply and for the first time recognized that he was a bit disgruntled. "I'm sorry," she said hesitantly. "If I'm imposing, I'll leave, but I just thought after the other day . . ."

56

"No, really, it's all right," he said as he massaged his neck nervously. "I'm glad to see you."

"You didn't call," said Jessica with a question in her voice.

Their eyes met in an anguished reunion until he forced himself to look away. "I—I wasn't sure if I should," he said softly. "You know, living out here alone. I began to think I'd imagined . . ."

"You did not," Jessica said spiritedly. "You're a man who knows exactly what's going on. Now, if you've had a change of heart, I'll understand. I mean it was all rather sudden."

"No change of heart," he said tenderly as he gave in to his full rush of emotion and lifted her chin to look her in the eye. "After reflection, I just didn't think a woman like you could really be interested in a life like this."

"Maybe that's something we should find out," she said with a little laugh. "But you know that's a two-way street, Mr. Farley, president of Acme Enterprises. I know you don't spend all of your time out here."

His eyes flashed with surprise and for an instant Jessica thought he was going to be angry. Then his expression relaxed, the smile reappearing on his rugged features.

"Nosy little lady, aren't you?" he said in real admiration.

"I guess you could say that," she said as she took his arm and began to walk with him to the house. "I may be crazy enough to lose my head with a total stranger, but I'm smart enough to find out who he is before I really make a mess of things."

"Says who?" Clay laughed.

"Says me!"

She stood before him pert and challenging and he knew he would never be able to resist her again, nor did he want to. "We'll see about that," he said huskily as he pulled her close and touched her lips lightly with his own. "Did you come prepared to spend the night?"

"No!" she said haughtily as she laughed and pulled away from him. "I came to get a program for the Brownies and that's what I'm going to do."

"Is that so?" he said. "Well, before you can do that, you may have to sweeten my mood a bit."

"I'm not in the habit of chasing men who ignore me," she said impudently.

"So who's ignoring?" he asked as they went through the door of the cabin and he gave her bottom a playful swat.

"Horrible man," she laughed. "Have I allowed myself to be led into a fate worse than death after all?"

"I hope so," he said wickedly as he pulled her close again and kissed her hungrily. Gone was the jesting as their bodies immediately ignited, and within moments they were clinging to each other in mutual desire and need.

"Don't deny me anything," he whispered. "I don't think I could stand it again."

"I won't," she said softly. Then she pushed him away with a little laugh. "But first things first. Let me get my video equipment out of the hot sun and maybe we should go on and get the taping out of the way too."

"Okay," he said with a sigh as he traced her features with his finger and gave her another gentle kiss. "I guess we have plenty of time."

"I hope so," she answered as she moved playfully away from him and he followed her to the car. Again neither of them reflected seriously on the phenomenon that seemed to occur so naturally between them. It was truly as if they had known each other for years and were completely comfortable in that existence whenever the passions of their bodies called.

She struggled with the equipment and he helped her, a rather baffled expression on his face. "What in the world do you think you're going to do with all of this?"

"Just get some pictures for my Brownies," she said with a big smile as she slid the straps of the tape deck over her shoulder and felt its leather case bouncing snugly on her hip. "I know none of them have ever seen anything like this."

He shook his head. "And what makes you think they will understand . . . ?"

"You're going to explain it to them," she said brightly as she flipped on the camera for outdoor use and checked to be sure her battery was good.

"You just said a moment ago that I wasn't going to be in it."

"Well, not necessarily in the pictures," she said as she hoisted the lightweight camera to her shoulder and began to focus on the white beehives to correct her light balance. "But you can at least explain a little bit of it, can't you?"

"I knew it," he said with an amused grimace as he openly appreciated the way the straps outlined her breasts when she lifted the camera. "I don't think I should trust you for one minute."

"Paranoid again," she said with a bright smile. But

her stomach turned a little flip-flop all the same as she squirmed a bit beneath his gaze. For the first time she began to grow a little uncomfortable about her deception no matter how innocent or legitimate she felt it to be. She was, she assured herself, going to use it with the Brownies, and for something else only if the opportunity arose. This wasn't the same as actually recording for the station like an assignment on something.

The little light in the lens went out, telling her she was ready to tape, and she began to unwind the cord on the boom microphone while she looked around trying to decide where to begin. The equipment, although compact, was a bit unwieldy, but she had always found it very simple to use after lugging around the much more sophisticated and heavier equipment used at the television station.

Clay watched all of this with a real degree of fascination. "You handle that stuff like you really know what you're doing," he said.

She stopped for a second and managed to stifle a little gasp. She looked away and deliberately answered a bit absently while she feigned an intense interest in her procedures. "It's fairly simple," she said, "once you get the hang of it. Besides, I do this all the time."

She waited expectantly, assuming he would follow up on the comment, and prepared to make a clean sweep of the whole thing. But for some reason her words seemed to glance away from him as he began to carefully examine the microphone that she had handed to him while she aimed the camera and prepared for a trial run. A little pang went through her as she realized for the first time he had never once indicated an interest in what she did for a living.

But then she blushed as his nearness began to affect her. She felt his hands grazing her hips when he examined the tape deck and felt his eyes traveling over her breasts when they followed the cord plugged into the camera. "You know, I'll bet we could do all kinds of things with this and the equipment I have inside." His eyes were pools of fascination.

Sinkingly Jessica remembered the mass of electronics in the corner of his living room and acquiesced to the thought that fate was in charge of this situation.

Taking a deep breath she moved haltingly toward the porch. Her steps set all of the video paraphernalia into motion against her body and again she could sense his appreciation and amusement. "Yes, especially if you have a color TV," she said as she nodded her head in the direction of the house. "We could use it to monitor the color, since the camera lens only shows me black and white while I'm shooting."

"Sure, why not, but listen, why don't you let me help you with some of that?" His voice was a bit impatient as he noticed little beads of perspiration on her upper lip. He licked his own lips as he thought of kissing her again and imagined how exciting it might be to hold her when her body had warmed to such a degree in response to his own.

"No, really, I'm used to it," she said hastily, and again waited for him to pick up on her comments.

"Okay, suit yourself," he said as he looked at the microphone again. "You know, it's amazing. This thing picks up sound and everything, doesn't it?" He was almost like a child making a new discovery. His

61

mind obviously was far too busy assimilating the information he was gathering to react to her comment in a more usual way. "Does the television have to be brought out, or what?"

"We probably won't be able to use it on the outside," she said. "Unless you've got an extra-long extension cord or convenient power sources around those areas I want to shoot."

"Oh, sure, we can work that out," he said as his enthusiasm finally overtook him. "You know I think this is going to be a lot of fun."

She laughed. "Well, I'm just amazed that you haven't already got this equipment—"

"Just never thought of it," he said honestly. "I rarely turn the television on because the reception is lousy out here. I've preferred my short-wave radio and stereo for entertainment, but I can see all sorts of possibilities now. With this you could be in control of everything and watch just what you wanted to."

"That's right," she said sinkingly as she realized his attitude hadn't changed one iota. He had just found another way to expand his self-contained universe.

He was off now, his virile, muscular frame bounding toward the barn, and soon returned with a hundred-foot heavy-duty extension cord. "This should take care of it," he said. His eyes were bright and shiny with excitement. Jessica felt herself starting to sag as suddenly her original idea seemed more than a little farfetched now.

"Honestly," he said as he noticed her change in demeanor, "it's crazy for you to lug all of that equipment until we get this set up."

His hands began to tug knowledgeably at the straps

as he took the camera from her. Quickly he divested Jessica of the equipment, laying it carefully on the porch while her body sang inwardly and outwardly to the intimacy of his touches. He pulled out a big white handkerchief and tenderly wiped the sweat from her brow, pausing for a tender nibble of her lips as he took her arm and propelled her toward the steps. "There. Isn't that better?"

"Yes," she said a little hesitantly. "I had no idea that this would turn into such a production."

Her eyes flickered a bit and she inwardly admitted that she hadn't counted on the strain of her deception either. It was obvious that she had to find a way to lead into a conversation that would convince him that he should willingly share his knowledge—with everyone, not just a group of Brownies. Then she could extricate herself from this situation gracefully and hopefully not lose the relationship with him as well. She realized, though, that that was actually too much to expect from such a brief encounter, and she wished desperately she hadn't begun this in the first place.

"That stuff was a lot heavier than you thought," he said knowingly as he saw the tiny lines of fatigue and worry creeping into her face. "Sit there for a moment and I'll get you something cool to drink. Later we'll bring the television out and hook it up."

"Okay," she said as the last of her enthusiasm ebbed away. She couldn't care less if she ever put any of this on tape now. She was filled with a self-loathing so punctuated with disgust that she was close to angry tears.

The simple thing to do would have been to blurt out the truth. Tell him what her intentions had actually been in coming here with her video recorder, but somehow she couldn't bring herself to do that. It was almost as if a fear she couldn't identify had paralyzed her until she defiantly lashed back in self-defense. *If he weren't so wrapped up in himself, he would have figured it out by now,* she fumed to herself. *You'd think he would at least wonder what I do for a living. . . .*

"Why the sad face?" asked Clay as he returned with a glass of iced herb tea.

She looked at him for a long moment. "It's a long story," she said weakly.

"So tell me about it," he said as he flopped on the grass near her. His strong thighs were plainly outlined in tight jeans belted beneath a chambray shirt that strained against the muscles of his back and, as usual, his square, handsome face was enhanced by a winning smile.

She heaved a big sigh and plunged in, forcing herself to ignore his more obvious physical charms. After all, this was exactly the opening she had just been complaining to herself about. She lifted her eyes and met his squarely. "I guess I was still hoping I could get you to be a little more open about your life-style." She swallowed as she searched for just the right words. "Let me tell others about it, maybe like a documentary or something."

"So why the frown?" he asked, honestly amazed. He gestured expansively as a lock of hair fell down on his forehead, giving him a charming hint of boyishness. "I can't wait to do this now if for no other reason than to play with that video equipment. And if it helps your Brownies, great!"

"I know," she said as she tried to quell a wild inner lashing, "but I had something a little more—"

"We'll do whatever you want," he said as he reached over to nuzzle her cheek.

She took another big breath and decided to try to get out of this rather than confess her professional motive. "Well, now that I'm thinking about this, maybe it isn't such a g-good idea," she stammered. "I mean, now that I'm into it, this is probably going to be over the heads of the kids and the light's not—"

"Not on your life," he said incredulously. His jaw clenched ever so slightly. "You talked me into this with what I might add were some pretty persuasive arguments." He added the last as a little aside with an appropriate lift of his eyebrows and another full perusal of her body. "And I want to see how all of that video equipment works."

Obviously it was out of her hands. "Okay, if you insist," she said with a sigh.

"Now, what in heck's gotten into you," he said as he realized she actually was hedging on this. "I'm beginning to think I don't understand you after all."

"I know," she said. "And that's the problem."

"And what is that supposed to mean?" he asked.

"Oh," she said with an airy sigh as she squirmed again beneath his gaze, and owing to an admitted lack of courage opted again for a half truth rather than a full confession. "Just that maybe this was something I thought up because subconsciously I wanted to see you again."

"And now that you know your fondest wishes are going to come true," he said with a decidedly exaggerated grin, "you think there's no need to continue with your maidenly ploy."

"You wish," she said as she responded to him in spite of her dark thoughts. His infectious good humor laced with such obviously naughty overtones was simply irresistible.

"I do wish," he said as his eyes crinkled mischievously. "But more than that, I'm getting used to the idea that I want you to begin to seriously think about our life-styles and this is probably as good a way as any to begin." There was an unmistakable air of roguishness about him now.

"I know where you're coming from," she said in ridiculous coy menace, knowing full well how corny the words she was about to utter were going to be. "You just want to handle my equipment. I can tell. That's all you have in mind."

"Very perceptive," he said in like response. "Now, what do you say we get on with it." He reached out and boisterously gave her a quick kiss while his hands roamed teasingly over her body.

Jessica responded unthinkingly as she reveled in the warmth of his touch. "Cad," she laughed.

For a second his eyes lingered on her face, which was flickering with just the tiniest hint of indecision as he dwelled on the softness of her lips and cleavage. "Shall we?" he asked with a bit of a sacrificial sigh as he moved reluctantly toward the camera.

Oh well, why not, thought Jessica as she smiled at his conflicting reactions. She had come this far and he seemed so receptive now. If she had to, she could always erase the tape and in the meantime he might be right. Obviously she was still powerfully attracted to him, and they both had a lot of things to think about. This might be a help.

Clay was definitely like a child with a toy as they began to tape a few moments later. He soon took over the operation of the video recording equipment and went gleefully from one end of his compound to the other. He rigged the color TV and fussed and fiddled with it and the camera tape deck until Jessica actually began to grow a bit weary of the whole thing. But he also gave an elaborate explanation of everything and openly hammed into the camera when Jessica was taping. Consequently the procedure degenerated into laughing and loving camaraderie until finally Jessica collapsed on the porch steps in utter exhaustion.

"You know, this has been a lot of fun," she said as Clay deposited the last of the equipment on the porch. "But I think I know more about the way you live up here now than I ever wanted to know."

He gave her an appraising look as he noticed the sun glinting on her hair. He obviously chose his next words for effect. "So does that mean maybe I've proven I'm not quite the nut you thought I was?"

"Oh, I don't know about that," she said with her usual candor.

"Watch your tongue, woman," he said in a playfully menacing voice. "Is that any way to talk to a man who watched over and protected you with his life?"

She colored as memories of their first meeting came quickly to mind. "I was perfectly all right," she said with a little toss of her head.

"Says who?" he shouted as his strong arms reached out and scooped her to him in one swift motion. In seconds he had her completely immobilized as she squirmed beneath the weight of his body and felt the coolness of the grass on her neck. "Now who's going to save you?" he asked.

"Who says I want to be saved?" she whispered as suddenly her body began to sing against his and her voice grew husky with emotion. In an instant she wanted him, and now that seemed more important than anything else—as if the moment might be snatched from her forever unless she took advantage of it right now.

"I like that thought," he growled as his lips began to move over her features until they hungrily captured her mouth and their bodies melted into one long rapturous caress. With a determined groan he rolled to the side and gently helped her to her feet only to sweep her bodily into his embrace again. He lifted her and easily carried her up the steps while their eyes glazed with need and mutual passion. Their lips met again and again after nibbling and devouring each other over fiery tracks. He tightened his embrace and curved her body close to his as they moved down the hall toward the bedroom.

In heavenly communion they lay close together as he tenderly pulled her clothes away and slowly began a feast of sensation over her entire body. In easy, wanting acquiescence Jessica pulled her bra away and reached to undo his shirt. Her hands were buried in the resilient curly hair on his chest and she reveled in a floating out-of-body ecstasy as his hands and tongue scoured her and left her trembling in need.

Her breasts tempted him as he reached in hunger to suckle her thrusting nipples while she ran her hands over the rippling muscles in his back and shivered from the titillation of the brush of hair on his chest. She followed the dark arrow of its track and gloried in his gasp when she reached to give a sweet massage of her own. He answered with soft moans as his lips tracked lower and lower until she reveled in the waves of desire created by the magic of his caresses.

It was a tender meeting when he rose above her and she welcomed him eagerly, almost as if they were two primitives who had just discovered the real source of love. In an ancient rhythm he loved her and cherished her. His hands traveled over her breasts and his lips again succored the softness of her rosy nipples until at last the frenzy of their need drove them in wild abandon. In an anguished tender surrender they clasped each other in a final breathless crescendo and then listened quietly as the roar of their hearts dimmed to a whisper and they found themselves mutually soothing each other.

Within five minutes Jessica was filled with regret as she realized how little she knew about this man and acknowledged how totally wanton she had been in her need for him. A little shiver went through her and Clay immediately sensed it. He rose above her and tenderly turned her face to meet his own. He immediately understood as she fastidiously reached for the sheet to cover herself. "No, don't," he said as he caressed her brow softly. "Sometimes a moment is meant to last a lifetime, and that's what I think this could be." He reached down to tenderly circle her breast and delved deeply to erase the anguish in her eyes. "Fortunately, though, it doesn't have to because there's going to be a whole lot more of them."

"Isn't that a little too trusting and hopeful?" she asked, her words tinged with spite and self-derision.

"I'm the most trusting man in the world," he said as he continued to look deeply into her eyes. "The only problem with that is that there aren't too many people in this world who deserve my trust."

"And now you know me well enough after a little hop in the bed to—"

"I've known you forever," he said with a sage smile, not allowing her to finish while his hands continued to caress her. "It's taken me a couple of days to understand it, but the link was there from the moment I set eyes on you."

Now Jessica was really alarmed. She felt like a penniless child looking through the glass of a candy shop window. She had never been loved in such a gently fulfilling way, and now in heart-shattering sickness she suddenly knew she would never get to sample the true delights of the relationship he had just offered. "Clay," she said hesitantly. "There's something I have to tell you. . . ."

"There's nothing you have to tell me," he said as he reached to caress her again. "What we just said to each other is all that I ever need to know."

"But we have so much to talk about," she sputtered.

"All in good time," he said gently. "I know everything can be worked out between us. I've never been so positive of anything in my life."

"How can you be so positive about this and so negative about everything else?" she asked in frustration.

"Simple," he answered. "I'm basically an honest, decent guy who somehow had a flair for advertising. Writing copy and coming up with promotional schemes just seemed to come natural to me, but after a while it all seemed to be so much ado about nothing."

"Well, that's no reason to leave the world of the living," said Jessica as she felt herself relaxing and warming to the sincerity of his words. Maybe, after all, they would get this worked out.

He responded immediately to the jest in her words and eyes. "No," he said. "The fantasy side of advertising has always been fun. It's the down and dirty side that gets to you when you see so-called civilized people at their very worst."

"But don't you think you've overreacted?"

"No," he said resolutely. "I learned the hard way not to let anyone walk on me, which wasn't easy because I trusted everyone—especially women."

"I can tell," she said as she traced a nipple through the hair on his chest and her voice dropped conspiratorially.

"Are you challenging me?" he asked in mock consternation.

"Not on your life," she said, "but I still don't understand where you are coming from."

"I'm trying to tell you," he said as he tipped her chin up to look her squarely in the eye. "I have a very simple philosophy. I trust everyone until they prove they can't be trusted. If that happens, then I'd never trust them again."

Jessica's heart flipped and thudded resoundingly in her chest. Suddenly she wished she had not taped anything remotely connected with Clay or his life-style here in the wilderness. She breathed a sigh of relief, though, as she remembered that her videotape couldn't be used on the station equipment without a

71

real hassle, so she was home free so far as that was concerned when she finally told him her occupation. Somehow, though, she still felt she needed to find just the right opening to bring that up. Her common sense told her she'd better do it and do it now. But everything else inside of her was quaking with fear and it told her this wasn't the time.

"That doesn't sound like the shoot-first-and-ask-questions-later approach you seemed to have the other day," she said a little weakly as she tried to accent her words with a coy toss of her head.

"Oh, I wouldn't say that," he said as he looked at her a little ruefully. "I could have used a telescopic sight on the rifle and scared the raisins right out of you, but if you recall, I came down to definitely get a closer look."

She felt herself blush as she remembered him watching her through the binoculars while she labored over the tent. "You were just a cad, and you know it," she said as her spirit began to respond to him in the usual way. "I think this whole thing of you living out here by yourself in secret is a big sham. You don't want to live alone any more than I do."

"Not anymore," he said with a big grin. "At least you got that part right." He gave her a playful swat as he pulled her to her feet and began to retrieve their clothes.

As she shrugged into her shirt and began absently to button it he kissed her gently and pulled her into a warm embrace. "I'm not so sure I'm ready to get up after all," he said with a familiar huskiness.

Jessica laughed as she pulled on her jeans, rejecting her wild response to him as she looked out the window and saw the evening shadows beginning to fall. "I know," she said as she tucked in the tail of her shirt. "But I have to be getting back."

"Do you really?" he asked, his disappointment obvious.

"Yes, of course," she answered as she looked at him a little strangely. "Have you forgotten I have Janey to take care of?"

"No, of course not," he said as he began to get dressed too. "Listen, why don't you plan to come up with her and spend the weekend?"

Jessica stopped in mid-motion as she met his eyes. She felt herself reddening and hated herself for it as she recognized the funny feeling, almost like shame, that washed over her. "Oh, I couldn't bring her up here! Not just like that."

Clay was immediately perceptive and responded warmly. "No, of course not," he said. "Well, then how about if I come to see you?"

"Yes, that would be all right," said Jessica as she pushed her hair away from her face in an obviously evasive gesture. "It's just that I try to be careful. You know how little kids can get the wrong ideas so quickly."

"Now who's paranoid," he said as he came to her and gently raised her chin. He kissed her sweetly and Jessica again felt herself responding in a floodgate of emotion. "Look, why don't we do this?" he continued. "You come up and spend a day or two here and then I'll come to town."

"Are you sure?" asked Jessica, suddenly agonizingly serious.

"Like I told you a little while ago," he said as he

responded to the questions in her eyes. "I've never been so serious or more sure of anything in my life."

Or so wrong, thought Jessica fleetingly. Suddenly in the stark glare of unavoidable reality, given all of the circumstances as they stood now, she just knew this wasn't going to work out. And then, in bittersweet agony, she was more than grateful for these few moments of passion that they had just shared. They might very well have to last a lifetime.

CHAPTER FOUR

"Oh, my God, say it isn't so," Clay mumbled to himself as he came closer to a Little League baseball field the next day. Jessica was out in the middle of it with all of her Brownies, not twenty but forty at least. She was shouting directions, book in hand, apparently trying to teach them baseball. He looked back to his four-wheel drive, which he had parked on the edge of the field, and scratched his head in amused consternation. "Jessica!" he called, hoping he could be heard over the uproar of the kids. "Jessica!" he shouted again as he drew closer to her.

Finally Jessica disengaged herself from the group of children surrounding her and looked in his direction. A funny look crossed her face as Clay advanced toward her and then her face burst into a happy smile. "Hi," she shouted back as he rapidly closed in on her. "I'm trying to get ready for a tri-community field day next week."

"And you're the baseball coach?" he laughed as he

arrived and reached out to give her an affectionate squeeze.

"Yeah," she said as she self-consciously squirmed away from him, obviously not wanting him to kiss her in front of her juvenile charges. "You want to make something of it?"

"Only if you do," he answered, instantly aware of the defensiveness shrouded in her joking manner. His eyes crinkled, leaving a happy web of tracks around them as his face lit up from the pleasure of seeing her and being near her again.

"So what brings you to town?" she asked as she obviously was looking for a safe topic of conversation in front of the multitude of curious young faces. "I didn't think you'd be coming in so soon."

"I missed you," he said simply as his eyes took in all of her attributes, attractively highlighted by the simplicity of her playclothes. He reached out to dab a wisp of perspiration from her face, which made her even more appealing, as he reacted to that vulnerability that seemed to cloak her when she was enmeshed in one of these ridiculous situations.

Within seconds the vibrations were twanging all about them as Jessica looked into his eyes and unconsciously reached to cover her heart in a protective gesture as the force of his magnetism once more swept her away. "It's only been a day," she said hesitantly.

"That's one day too many," he said firmly as he again reached out and scooped her close in a casual one-arm hug. "I barely slept last night thinking about us and how we can't waste another minute. I came down as soon as I could get away because we have to talk."

"Well, not here," said Jessica in a mild panic now. "I mean I've got to finish with these kids and then—" *Go to work,* she was going to say, but he didn't let her finish as he broke in.

"That's okay," he said jovially. "Just as long as I'm with you. Looks like you could use a little help anyway."

There was a definite tongue-in-cheek air about him now, and in spite of her tension Jessica found him completely irresistible. Gone now were the feelings of doubt and shame that had plagued her since leaving him the evening before. Every time she looked at Janey and thought of her impulsiveness and lack of control, not to mention her quasi-deception, she was wracked with feelings of panic and derision laced with a generous dose of longing and need. Now as Clay held her close she felt euphoric and curiously silly as little eyes in little expectant faces watched the two of them.

"Have you ever played baseball before?" he asked. "Do you know anything about it?"

She looked at him furiously as he retrieved the rule book from her hand and then she smiled in total confession.

He looked around the playing field and again took in the total number of kids there and gave her an exasperated look. "Yes, I know," he said as he jostled her affectionately and his face hinted at both incredulity and admiration. "If it's in a book, anyone ought to be able to do it!"

She joined him in chorus for the last few words and they both laughed. "Where have I heard that before?"

he said in true merriment as he gave her bottom a pat and quickly began to take over the whole procedure.

"Now, you and you and you," he said as he quickly designated three players, "spread out in the back so you can be fielders. Take a glove!"

"Mommy, who is this?" asked a miniature of Jessica who squinted up at him through freckles and glasses.

"Oh, this is Mr. Farley," said Jessica. She spoke rapidly and visibly grew nervous again. "He's just going to help Mommy out for a while."

"Was he going to kiss you?" she asked with a bit of a pout in her voice.

"No, of course not," said Jessica as she hurriedly scooted her child away. "Here, take this glove and you can go and play second base."

"But I want to bat," she wailed.

"Do as you're told," said Clay firmly. He was suddenly assailed with a strange impatience over the child's seemingly spoiled and brattish nature accompanied by Jessica's obvious vulnerability to her.

Janey responded with a shocked look.

"I mean, we won't be able to have a first-rate team without a super second baseman, now, will we?" he said in a much softer voice as he quickly relented from his tough stance and tried to win her over.

"Oh, who cares?" said Janey with a shrug as she walked away toward second base.

"I take it that was Janey," said Clay with a little grimace.

"Yes," said Jessica with a sigh. "I'm sorry. I guess I handled that badly."

"No problem," said Clay. "I'm sure we can mend the fences a little later." But inwardly he mused to himself as he sized up the situation. *It's Mother who has the problem,* he thought. *Not Janey.* Then he was curiously gratified to see Janey nonchalantly avoiding his eyes but nevertheless standing quite close to second base.

For the next two hours Clay helped Jessica put the kids through their paces and was struck by the uncanny natural ability that Jessica seemed to have for coaching this sport. She seemed to quickly size the kids up and compare their abilities with the needs and goals of the game, and it was amazing what was accomplished in such a short time. "I think you've got real possibilities here," he said as the last kids were being picked up by their parents. "But don't any of these kids have parents who could help you?"

"Yes, I suppose so," she said lamely, "but I just hate to bother people. I mean, I was the one who got myself into this."

"Still Supermom," he said softly as they looked into each other's eyes. "When are you going to learn that you don't have to be?"

"Probably never," she said with a little laugh. "I mean, you just can't shrug off responsibilities like that."

"Why not?" he asked with a grin. "Look at me. Here I am, the world's biggest corporate dropout back in town after only twenty-four hours."

"Oh, pooh, you haven't changed that much," she said as Janey came running toward them again.

"You want to bet?" he said. "I still think the only place to live is up on Owl Hill, but I think it might be fun to check out a little bit of the world again if you come along."

"Oh," she said, honestly surprised now by the change in him. "What do you have in mind?"

"Well, maybe for openers," he said with a twinkle in his eyes, "since you obviously are a reservoir of latent baseball talent just waiting to be discovered, how about going down to Dallas and taking in a Rangers game? They're hot right now."

"But that's more than a half a day away," she said, obviously alarmed. "It would mean staying overnight."

"Precisely," he said with a Cheshire-cat grin and undisguised anticipation etched all over his face.

"But I couldn't," she said as she quickly looked around to see if Janey was listening. "I mean . . ."

"Oh, you could work it out," he said confidently as he immediately grasped the source of her confusion. "As far as I'm concerned, Janey is welcome to come."

"Oh, no!" said Jessica quickly, cutting him off. "I mean . . . I've already told you this has to be handled very carefully, but that's not the only problem. You know I have to work too."

"It would probably be a weekend," he said patiently.

And again Jessica was newly aggravated as he showed no interest in her occupation, clearly assuming she had some nondescript office job or something. It seemingly never occurred to him to pick up on one of these opportunities and ask her what she did for a living.

"It's not that simple," she said as she impatiently pulled away from him and walked rapidly ahead. *Serves him right,* she thought as she glanced back covertly and noted the hurt look on his face. Then she was also instantly contrite, realizing how impossible she was being. After all, hadn't she, in spite of her anxiety, spent the entire night before dreaming of him and the hours they had spent together, longing for his touch and the special way he made love?

"I'm sorry," she said with a big sigh as she turned to face him and waited for him to reach her again. "I'm just a little edgy, I guess. Everything seems to have moved so fast."

"I understand," he said as he immediately responded to the anguish in her eyes. "I've caught you at an awkward time and this is new to both of us, you know. Maybe we both need to remember that."

"You're too good to be true," said Jessica as she melted into his body and felt the snugness of his embrace when his arm went around her again and they walked on in warm intimacy. "I'd love to see a big league baseball game. I've never been to one."

"You haven't?" he said in sudden exuberance. "I love going to baseball games. There's nothing like the excitement of actually being there."

"I'll bet," said Jessica with a touch of her old derisive spirit as she inwardly gloried in the tumbling feelings that rolled throughout her body from both the touch of his body and his spirit.

"Can I go too?" a pixieish voice asked.

Jessica and Clay looked at each other in confusion. "Not this time, Janey," said Clay before Jessica could speak. "Maybe a little later, though, when your mama says so," he added with a smile.

"Aw, shucks," she said petulantly. "I never get to go anywhere."

"That's not true," said Jessica firmly as she left Clay

81

to go to her daughter. "I spend nearly all of my free time with you. Think of all the things we do together. All the fun we have." Janey looked to the ground as Jessica stooped and raised the child's chin so they looked into each other's eyes. "Isn't that true, Janey?"

"Yes," said Janey, a little chagrined, as she obviously wished Clay weren't there watching.

But Clay was newly impressed with Jessica as he watched this exchange. There was obviously a very close and loving bond between these two, and contrary to his earlier impression on the ball field, Jessica was also a firm and fair disciplinarian and she and the child understood each other well. Touching as this was, he also recognized it as a possible formidable obstacle and tucked it away in his subconscious for careful consideration.

Moments later, though, they were all happily heading for Jessica's house and Janey was in her glory as she rode in Clay's four-wheel drive following her mother's car. With each bump she whooped in laughter and Clay began to feel a wonderful warmness for her which jelled perfectly with his feelings for her mother and gave him a marvelous sense of completeness.

As she drove toward her house, though, Jessica was a bundle of nerves. She couldn't deny how happy she was to see Clay again, but now, away from his physical presence, she was suddenly overly anxious. Her hands shook as they gripped the wheel and her breathing quickened as she thought again of Janey's discovery and initial comments concerning Clay. Now, as they neared her neat square natural-stone house set on a spacious lot beneath old shade trees and surrounded by a rustic picket fence, she worried ridiculously over what Clay would think of her modest home. She tried to remember what state of chaos the house was in after being assaulted by all those Brownies. But as Clay pulled up behind her with a snappy jerk to his brake and stepped down with a decided bounce in his step, she once again was pleased as he exuberantly reached up to help Janey down.

"Nice little place," he said happily as he reached to open the gate, which revealed a neatly mowed yard and old-fashioned flower beds. "Native stone that must be at least fifty or sixty years old . . ."

"Yes, I think so." Jessica laughed as they neared the porch. "Lately there have been so many things that need fixing that sometimes I think it's twice that old."

She fidgeted and met his eyes in confusion as she gratefully clung to these easy tidbits of small talk. She looked about for the note she had left on the front porch directing latecoming Brownies to the park and was suddenly perplexed over its being gone.

"Looking for something?" Clay asked.

"Yes," she said as she looked at him a little dazed, still suffering from the delayed effects his appearance was having upon her.

"This?" he asked with an inquisitive grin as he pulled the sheet of paper from his pocket.

"What are you doing with that?" she asked, still incapable of functioning at her normal astute level.

"How do you think I found you?" he asked as he gave her chin a little nudge. "And I didn't think you needed to announce to the world that the house was empty."

"But what if some others came late?" she asked, suddenly annoyed over his presumption.

"It was more than an hour late by then," he said as he openly enjoyed her heightened color and the touch of hauteur that she assumed so easily.

"I think you were a little presumptuous," she said as she opened the screen and fumbled with the lock, nevertheless feeling an insidious hint of laughter creeping into her voice.

"If you say so," he said with his usual good humor in these situations. "But you know a woodsman just can't deny his instincts."

"Is that so?" she said as they entered the small foyer of the house and went on into the sunny living room filled with plants and easy, comfortable furniture.

Janey followed them in, her arms loaded awkwardly with the baseball paraphernalia she had gathered from her mother's car and headed toward her room with a groan as Jessica pointed the way to her. "Isn't slavery against the law?" the child gasped as Clay and Jessica both laughed at her antics.

"Not for eight-year-old Brownies who want to play baseball," sang Jessica as she turned back to Clay.

Again she was struck by the handsomeness and nearness of his tanned body as he nonchalantly perused her and her surroundings in a perfectly relaxed way. She tried again to calm the little twinges that went through her as she worried over his reactions. When Janey dropped her burdens with a resounding thud and headed for the kitchen, it was a welcome distraction.

"So what do you think?" asked Clay as Jessica gave Janey a snack and sent her out to play. Then she nervously made the motions to entertain him. She couldn't believe how flighty she was over his unexpected visit as she reached for glasses and tried to think of what she had to offer. "About what?"

"Going to the baseball game in Dallas," he persisted.

"Oh, that," she said as she breathed a sigh of relief over the general tidiness of the house and the fact that there was cold wine and soft drinks in the refrigerator. "I'd have to give it some thought."

"What's to think about?" he said. His enthusiasm in anticipation of the event shaped his words as he joined her in the kitchen and then followed her back to the living room.

"Well," she said absently, not really thinking about what she was saying as she unconsciously fussed about the house straightening a pillow and pointing Clay to the couch. "Maybe I could get a story assignment out of it."

Clay looked at her strangely. "What are you talking about?"

Jessica's head snapped as she realized the moment of truth was here whether she was ready for it or not. She took a big breath and plunged on. "A news or feature assignment for KROY. That's what I do for a living. I'm a reporter."

She didn't flinch as she looked him in the eye and watched anxiously as a gamut of emotions turning from light to dark washed down over his face like a spilled palette of runny paints.

"What do you mean?" he asked as he searched for his voice and appropriate words. "Yesterday . . . All of that video equipment? You were . . . ?"

85

"No, not at all," she said quickly. "That was all my own equipment and I used it for just the reasons I told you. We could never use any of that tape at the station."

But Clay wasn't listening as he suddenly saw her in a new light. It was going to be the same deceitful experience with Clare all over again. He knew it, only this time it was so much worse.

"Well, actually," Jessica continued, deciding once and for all to make a clean breast of it as she mistook Clay's stunned silence as tolerance and an attempt to fully understand, "I did talk to Jim Reynolds about you, but he wasn't even faintly interested in a story about you."

"You were planning to do a story about me, to show everyone my hideaway?" His voice was incredulous as full comprehension finally settled into his mind.

"No, not unless you wanted me to," she cried as she realized now how he was reacting. "If you recall, I changed my mind about the whole thing, but you were the one who wanted to go on and do the taping."

"You said it was for your Brownies," he seethed.

"Yes, that's right," she said as she brushed her hair back anxiously. "But I also thought you had something unique to share. When I made attempts to explain, you were so wrapped up in your own interests that you just never picked up on it. Later it seemed as though I just couldn't find the right words."

"When will I ever learn?" he asked in sudden bitter self-derision. "You'd think by now I'd learn not to trust a woman, especially when she's being so—"

"Now, just a minute," flared Jessica as her usual spirit renewed itself once more. "I think you're having more than a little overreaction to this. If you had ever once asked me flat out what I do, I would have told you. But you never even thought of it."

He looked at her strangely, as if seeing her for the first time. Jessica knew her worst fears were about to come true. "And furthermore," she continued, knowing that the relationship had been little more than a gossamer web from the beginning and now it was irretrievably broken, "to begin with, you were the one who stuck your nose in my affairs. Any intelligent person with a shred of curiosity would have responded to that situation the same as I did."

"By coming out to my place with a video camera and recording—"

"Only for the reasons I told you about," she insisted. "I realized once I was there that I could never compromise the trust you had placed in me. If only you hadn't made me feel so paranoid about the whole thing."

"So where is the tape now?" he snarled.

"Over there," she said as she gestured to the VCR equipment in the corner. "I'd planned to erase it after . . ."

"I'll just bet you had," he said as he walked over to examine the equipment.

"Mommy, are you married again," said Janey's sad little voice as she looked into the room.

"No, Janey, of course not," said Jessica in a shocked voice as she walked over to her daughter and gave Clay a warning look. "Why ever would you ask that?"

"Well, it sounds like you're having the same kind of *discussions* that you used to have with Daddy."

Jessica gave Clay an anguished look and he looked

to the floor as he clenched his fists. The planes of his face squared into an angular grimace and for a moment Jessica thought she saw real concern and pain in his eyes.

"No, not at all. You go on and take your bath now," said Jessica to Janey. "Mr. Farley and I were just having a little disagreement and we didn't know we had gotten so noisy."

"Well, are the Brownies still going to get to see the tapes like you promised?" she asked as she gave Clay a menacing look.

"I guess that depends upon Mr. Farley," said Jessica as she met Clay's eyes. "If he's changed his mind about that, I think we would have to respect it."

Clay gave her an exasperated look as Janey prepared for her last shot. "Well, I guess maybe I can understand that," she said with a hint of a pout. "He does look pretty silly in them."

"Janey!" exclaimed Jessica, aghast at her daughter's rudeness.

"Silly," said Clay, a bit shocked.

"Well, maybe just a little bit," said Janey as she retreated from her mother's angry eyes.

"I think we'll talk about this later," said Jessica as she again pointed Janey in the direction of the bathroom.

"That's probably a good idea for everyone concerned," said Clay, now obviously subdued and apparently reconsidering.

Jessica was shaky as she got up from the crouch in which she had been addressing Janey. She looked into his eyes and was overwhelmed by her own confusion.

"She's already seen the tape, then," he said as he felt

that unfailing response to Jessica's vulnerability. The hint of an uncontrollable smile began insidiously to play about his face, alternately crinkling and then sobering the lines around his eyes. "And I look funny . . ."

"She's just a child," said Jessica hastily as she turned away from him, suddenly cognizant of the change of atmosphere that filled the room. She could feel everything relaxing and draining as all of the harsh words left her. Then, as the familiar vibrations telegraphing straight from his body to hers began to swirl, she could feel a hint of hope and suddenly she was glad this was out and over with.

"And I meant every word of it too," a little voice called out from down the hall as the bathroom door slammed and the lock clicked.

In mutual surprise Clay and Jessica whirled around and looked at each other and then simply gave in to the humor of the situation. "Does that mean this has become a family matter?" Clay asked as he continued to try to stifle an involuntary smile.

"It looks that way," said Jessica. "I'm sorry. She doesn't usually act this way."

"Well, I guess, considering everything, I really can't blame her," said Clay. "Do you think we can sit down and talk this out now like two sensible adults?"

"Is that what you truly want?" asked Jessica as she felt familiar patterns of warmth wafting up and washing over her heart with an outrageous heady buoyancy.

"That's what I want," he said as his eyes embraced her and left little doubt in her mind. "Let's take it from the top."

"Okay. After I get Janey to bed," she said. "Do you think you can stand a hot dog for dinner?"

"I can stand anything," he said firmly as he reached out to touch her face. "I think I've just proven that to myself."

They looked at each other for a very long moment, their eyes radiating the tenderness of his touch to her cheek, and then Jessica reached out for his hand. "Do you want to tell me about it?" she asked. "And satisfy my curiosity for good?"

His eyes were pools, rippled with little hints of indecision. Then he nodded his head with a little sigh. "Yes, I guess that's what it's really all about, isn't it?"

"I don't know. What do you mean?" Her face mirrored the puzzlement of her words.

"If we truly care for each other, then we should trust each other. Our lives, past and present, should be readily shared, and we should be capable of understanding and forgiving things that obviously weren't planned or premeditated."

"I'm glad you think that way," she said as she moved closer and met his lips softly with her own. But deep inside, beneath the soft waves that moved through her body as the result of his touch, a little cord of doubt knotted into a ball as she remembered her original videotaping concept of the day before.

With a moan Clay pulled her closer and devoured her lips with a savage, needing intensity. "Oh, Jessie," he breathed. "I want so much for this to be perfect. I can't live without you now."

"I know," she said as her heart raced and her blood pounded. "I do too."

In a second the forces between them had erupted

and the passion of their need was drawing them on, completely oblivious to the world around them as Clay scooped her into his arms and carried her toward the couch. Jessica's mind soared as everything around her became soft and sharp at the same time in a dreamy, sensory way. Sounds were acutely melodious and the air was filled with aromas of pleasures as her body responded in a happy, giving way. Clay's lips followed the familiar trail down her neck and reached to caress the soft skin above her bosom as she ran her hands through his hair in ecstasy and kissed his brow softly and urgently. In blinding need they pulled each other close, as if an uncontrollable frenzy demanded that their bodies be permanently melded into one. As Jessica felt the length of his body searing hers she wanted him over and under and through her all at the same time. Their lips met again and again in wild parrying demands until only the need for breath could break them apart.

"Oh, Clay," breathed Jessica as his glazed eyes mirrored the burning embers of her own. "I've never wanted anyone so much as I want you." As Jessica's heart beat beneath his and reached out to capture his soul she knew these moments of ecstasy could never be denied when they were offered by this man.

"Oh, Jessie. I need you so," Clay whispered huskily. "Why don't we—" But before he could finish the chimes of the doorbell rang out and the mood was shattered.

"Yoo-hoo, anybody home?"

"Oh, my gosh," cried Jessica in panic. "My mother. I nearly forgot!"

As befuddled as she, Clay looked on in confusion,

unable to speak as he tried to free himself from the wild bonds of his physical passion.

In a second Jessica also remembered Janey in the bathroom taking a bath and suddenly she was overcome with a shame more debilitating and mortifying than any she had ever known. As her mother rapped on the screen door and began to come in, Jessica suddenly felt like a naughty schoolgirl who knew she had gone too far and was about to be caught in the worst possible way.

In blinding perception Clay fully realized what was happening and he felt helpless as he watched the confusion and panic play over Jessica's face. As she looked at him fleetingly while rapidly adjusting her clothes and going to greet her mother, he could feel her self-derision reaching out to touch him and he knew she suddenly detested his very presence.

"Come in, Mom," she called. Her voice was fluttery and it took her mother only a second to understand the situation. "Would you believe I almost forgot," Jessica went on rapidly. "Oh, this is Clay Farley," she said as her mother entered the room and instantly gave Clay a wide smile that was obviously beaming with approval.

"I forgot," said Jessica to Clay now. "I'm going on a special assignment up around Eureka Springs and Fayetteville. Can you believe my news director wants a feature on the scenic spots in northern Arkansas. . . ." She was so flustered and nervous that words poured out of her in a wild and almost inane jumble as Clay wished fervently that he could somehow ease the situation for her.

"Anyway," continued Jessica after a big breath that

92

did much to settle her, "Janey is going to spend a few days with Mom and she's come over to pick her up."

"Marvelous," said Clay to Jessica's mother in his most cordial and suave voice. "I'm certainly pleased to meet you. I bet you have a wonderful time with Janey."

"Oh, we certainly do," she answered, completely impressed with him now.

"Clay was just giving me a hand with the baseball practice," said Jessica, as she obviously was still trying to justify his being there, and in motions dripping with guilt hoped her mother saw this as strictly a casual situation. "Janey's just taking her bath."

"Well, go and see to her, dear. I'm sure Mr. Farley can keep me company for a few moments."

"She hasn't had dinner," said Jessica hastily, as if it were absolutely necessary to make herself wallow in yet one more thing so she could make herself feel more guilty.

"Don't worry about that. I think we can take care of it," her mother called as she continued to give Clay a happy appraising look after Jessica disappeared down the hallway toward the bathroom.

Then she turned to Clay as she lowered herself onto the couch. "I'm so glad you're giving Jessica a little help," she said conspiratorially. "Baseball yet, for heaven's sake. I keep telling her she's trying to do too much."

They chatted amicably and easily for the next few minutes and Clay found himself warming to the older woman in an extremely natural way. When Jessica reappeared with Janey ten minutes later, she was still a little flustered, but Clay and Mrs. Sharp were obviously friends.

"Now, you go on and have a good time," she said as she gave Jessica and Clay a happy nod while reaching for Janey's hand.

"Oh, Clay just stopped in for a moment," said Jessica hastily. "He's only—"

"Of course, I understand," her mother answered. "I can't tell you how much I enjoyed chatting with you," she continued as she turned to Clay, "and I certainly hope we'll be seeing more of you."

"So do I," Janey chimed in as she hoisted up her small suitcase. "And don't forget. I still want to go with you two to the baseball game . . ."

"Janey!" said Jessica.

Her mother couldn't hide her instant approval. "Sounds like fun," she said as they descended the steps. Then in a more appropriate motherly tone she added, "It's about time that you began to go out, Jessica."

CHAPTER FIVE

Janey and her grandmother were gone for several minutes before Jessica could turn to face Clay again. "Oh, my God," she wailed as she looked at him angrily. "I've never been so mortified in my life!"

"I don't know why," said Clay gently. He had waited in helpless but perceptive silence, feeling every ray of her anger and derision. "You're a big girl now and your mother knows that."

"I know," she said, her voice watery with tears and frustration, "but, my God, I forgot all about Janey. What if she had come out here?"

"So she would have seen two people making love."

"Is that all you can say?" she asked incredulously. "A child might be totally traumatized by something like that. I have responsibilities and I just can't allow something like that to happen."

"I understand," he said as he moved to loosen the tight ball of her body from her criss-crossed, grasping arms. "I didn't mean that the way it sounded. Certainly we need to be careful of Janey's reactions, but I don't understand why you're so skittish about introducing me to your mother and acknowledging our relationship."

"For Pete's sake, we just met each other," said Jessica. "What would Mother think about that?"

"She doesn't know that," he said as he began to feel a bit annoyed. "Does this mean that I am to be relegated to a distant acquaintance or something in front of your family?"

"No, no," said Jessica, still completely confused by her reaction and unable to deny the terrible feelings of guilt she was experiencing. "I for some reason just can't quite cope with this. It's as if suddenly I'm doing something terribly wrong."

Immediately contrite now over his own aggravation, Clay pulled the hard knot of her body into his arms. "How can you say something so beautiful and perfect as what we experience when we see or touch each other is wrong?"

"I don't know," she said through muffled tears as she buried her head in his shoulder. "But I can't deny it either."

"You're free," said Clay as he held her away from him and forced her to meet his eyes. "You only have to answer to yourself."

"That's not so," she said with a little of her usual vigor. "There are other people I have to think about."

"But they don't want you to live a cold and barren life, wearing yourself out, denying yourself love, and trying to do everything by yourself. Your mother was delighted to see you with someone, and I can tell she worries about you the same way I do."

96

"Well, you certainly don't waste any time," she said as an involuntary smile began to play over her face, crinkling crazily through drying tears. She could feel her body softening beneath his gaze and touch. "You obviously won her over in less than five minutes."

"I'm glad you noticed," he said as he responded with his usual candor. "For a while there I thought you had missed that."

"Well, when you leave the gun home," she said with an edge of humor in her voice, "and you don't walk in scaring the wits out of someone, I can see where an unsuspecting, trusting person might react in that way to you."

"Still the ungrateful hussy," he said with a feigned menace as he pulled her close again. "Do you know how hard that ground was that night?"

"Yes," she said in real memory. "My body is still sore from it."

"And you had pine needles," he said as he began to tickle her ribs, sending her into outrageous whoops of laughter while trying vainly to defend herself.

"Stop," she gasped. "I can't stand any more tonight. If my mind has to conjugate anything else, it's going to explode."

"Conjugate?" he asked, puzzled.

"Yes," she said with a shrug. "Maybe that's a poor choice of word, but my brain has run the gamut of emotions today. First work, trying to keep everything straight there when Jim Reynolds, my news director, is on one of his highs, then Janey and the Brownies, trying to figure out how to coach baseball and now you . . . and . . . I needed to go and get squared away for the assignment."

"Enough, enough," he said, laughing. "You couldn't make order out of all of that anyway, and it just proves that you need to relax and pick a few priorities."

"Such as?" she asked teasingly as she finally felt all vestiges of her earlier anxiety falling away under the magic of his nearness and rationale.

"How about picking up where we left off a few moments ago?" he murmured softly. "The coast is clear, isn't it?"

"No," she said seriously as something tightened within her again and she knew she was not yet completely free of those earlier guilt feelings. "I don't think it would be quite the same."

"Wanna bet?" he teased.

"No," she said as she began to feel insidiously those stirrings that just thinking about being with Clay created. She grasped for some safer alternative. "Maybe this would be a good time to discuss baseball."

He stopped in mid-motion and looked at her incredulously. "I don't believe you," he said. "Leave it be. You don't have to do everything in one night."

"Then you'd probably better leave," she said sadly. "I'm just not up to—"

"No. I've got it," he said exuberantly. He grabbed her hand before she could speak and was pulling her toward the door. "C'mon. I'm going to take you out cruising. I haven't done that since I was in high school, and then we'll go to the ice cream parlor. That was something I always did with my best girls."

"Cruising?" she said.

"Yeah, you know, when you give your car a spit and

polish shine and then you go out and tool along Main Street on Saturday night."

"But you don't have a spit and polish shine on that thing out there," she said teasingly.

"So we'll just be a cool and chic older generation," he said airily, "coming to town from the hills."

"You're outrageous," she said, but suddenly she was captivated with his young-at-heart spirit and it sounded like a wonderful thing to do.

"After you," he said as she reached for a sweater. "We'll even have open-air cross-ventilation."

"Shabby," she said as she skipped down the stairs. "I can guarantee you that this will cost you the biggest banana split in town."

"You've got it," he said. "But first I'm going to show you this town as I see it, and then I'm going to tell you why I live out there on Owl Hill."

"All right," she said as she paused for a second. "I think that's exactly what you should do."

"Well, I'm glad we finally agreed on something," he said. He feigned relief as he helped her into his sturdy four-wheel drive. The grin on his face was infectious and Jessica didn't know when she had last felt so giddy as a result of giving in to such an outlandish whim. But as the truck roared to life she covertly examined Clay's handsome profile and wondered again at the many puzzling facets of this man who had so thoroughly captured her heart in such a very short time. Again she felt the impulse to retreat as everything practical in her gave out a resounding warning. But when he turned and met her troubled eyes, every doubt dissipated and she knew she wanted more than anything to go cruising downtown with this handsome, enigmatic man. She only wished her hair were in a ponytail to complete the nostalgic feelings she was experiencing.

"Now, this is the life," said Clay as he revved the motor and in general made a spectacle of them as they traveled down the main street of town.

"For someone who fancies himself a secretive recluse, you certainly are turning into a showoff," said Jessica. She laughed as he tooted his horn at a passing motorist.

"I'm not a secretive recluse," said Clay. "I'm just a man who has found his peace."

"A lonely peace," said Jessica.

"Yes," he said, pursing his lips and giving her a somber look.

"Why?" It was obvious that she meant to hold him to his earlier promise.

"Hmm, I did mention that, didn't I?" he said with a smile.

"You did."

"Well, it's a long story, but not really all that earth-shattering. It began in that building over there."

Jessica followed his gesture to a building that housed Acme Advertising.

"I built a good business based on trust and truth. And I had a partner, Clare Simpson—"

"A woman," said Jessica, suddenly tense.

"Not too many men have the name Clare," he said with a little smile. He couldn't believe how much her hint of jealousy pleased him.

Jessica gave him an insolent look.

"Anyway, it was no big deal," he said. "She was my partner. A good friend from college introduced us originally. That was back in the days when women were fighting to be recognized as capable executives, and I gave her a chance."

"No hanky-panky?" Jessica asked insistently.

"My word of honor," he said seriously as he reached out to touch her hand.

"Oh, not that it really matters," said Jessica hastily when she realized how proprietary she was sounding. "I mean, it would certainly be your business and probably to be expected in such a situation."

"Now who's stereotyping?" he asked teasingly. "Would you automatically think that if my partner were a man?"

"Well, obviously she was involved in some terribly traumatic thing that happened to you, so I'd just logically think—"

"Wrong," he said firmly. "She certainly did have something to do with my present philosophy and existence, but not for the reasons you would assume. Very simply, I trusted her, gave her authority, and extended every opportunity to her, never once putting her down because she was a woman even when she made a couple of screwball mistakes. I guess, though, because she was a woman, I never understood that she could be even more ambitious and deadly than some men I know."

"So what happened?" Jessica asked as wisps of gossip having to do with this suddenly began to emerge in her mind.

"Well, I had one rule about representing our accounts. Integrity was never compromised. Whatever we did, we never lied. Our commercials were honest and I dealt only with reputable people."

"So?" said Jessica as the city lights whirled past them and the cool evening breeze felt good on her warm brow.

"So obviously this doesn't always work in the company's best monetary interests. Clare saw opportunities to make bigger bucks by bending a word or innuendo here and there and at first I allowed her to charm me into it until the Napa account came along."

"Napa?" queried Jessica.

"Yeah, that's the big company that palmed off millions of dollars of inferior products to third-world companies—products that had been outlawed here, including non-flame-retardant children's clothes."

Jessica gasped as she remembered and immediately felt a natural mother's protective instinct as she thought of Janey in such garments.

"Anyway, it was a million-dollar-plus account and I turned them down cold. It was obvious that they wanted the integrity of my business to cleanse their own."

"Gutsy," said Jessica in real admiration. "But surely they wouldn't have that much trouble finding someone else for that kind of money."

"Right you are," he said with a weary grimace. "And that's when the trouble started. A few years before, we had allowed our company to go public to raise some needed capital for another ambitious project and Clare was so incensed over my decision, because among other things it might also have meant a foot in the door to the big guys in New York on Madison Avenue, that she actually called an emergency stockholders' meeting and tried to remove me from my own company!"

"You're kidding," said Jessica.

"No, I'm not," he said tightly. "And she didn't do it overnight either. She did this over a matter of months by going secretly behind my back while acting like sweetness and light to my face. She left me no alternative but to crush her with out-and-out strong-arm corporate power. The whole process left me so disgusted that I ultimately pulled in my resources, bought her and the other stockholders out, at a pittance, I might add, because by then they had thoroughly damaged the credibility of the company and reestablished on a much smaller and less ambitious scale."

"But that's no reason to leave the world," said Jessica.

"It is when you're faced with one unavoidable and unalterable fact."

"What?" asked Jessica as she inwardly gave in to a silly surge of relief that it hadn't been love that had stricken him down.

"You simply can't trust people. I mean *no one!* No matter what your own convictions and actions are, you've got to always be on your guard. Someone is always waiting to cut you down."

"And you think living up on Owl Hill will prevent that?" asked Jessica as she honestly tried to understand what he was saying.

"No," he said. "But life on Owl Hill is a constant challenge. Facing nature's law every day has better prepared me to handle the harsher realities of dealing with people in the city. In the process I discovered this incredible state of mind. There is such a feeling of accomplishment when everything works, and it means something. The beans I grow and the honey the bees

103

make actually sustain life. And it's all there in one little perfect place in the universe completely under my control."

"And you don't want anything or anyone mucking it up, right?"

"Yes, that's about right," he said as the city lights played over his face and he looked into her eyes. "Not unless it's something or someone who belongs there too."

"Are you listening to yourself?" asked Jessica, ignoring the unspoken invitation to intimacy of his last words. "How can you expect the world to change if people like you aren't willing to come out and slug it out day after day with people like Napa?"

"Because that way of thinking is futile. Only idealists with rose-colored glasses think that way and once they've experienced and understood basic reality they either join up with the down and dirty just to survive or they retreat into some existence that shields them from it."

"That's not true," said Jessica spiritedly. "What about all of those people who are constantly out fighting for this cause or that?"

"They honestly enjoy the adversity of it," he said with a sigh. "That's the conclusion I've come to. As a reporter you enjoy it too. I don't. I want peace and accomplishment in an atmosphere I can control."

"Sounds like a copout to me," said Jessica outspokenly. Actually she was more than a little annoyed with him.

His head snapped as he realized the sympathy and understanding he had just assumed would be forthcoming from this woman who had stirred him so and

'I'm not real sure," she said. "It may be just an-
[oth]er one of Jim's whims. He took a trip not long ago
[an]d came back raving about this terrific Italian restau-
[ra]nt out in the boonies near Fayetteville in a tiny place
[ca]lled Tonitown."

"Mary Maestri's," said Clay with real enthusiasm.

"You've heard of it?" said Jessica.

"Everybody who loves Italian food who has ever
[b]een to that area has heard of it," he said. "People
[fr]om all over the country go there. It's one of the
[g]reatest word-of-mouth success stories in the country
[b]ecause it literally sits out in a field on a highway
[c]rossroads and you'd never find it unless someone told
[y]ou about it."

"It sounds like you should be doing this story," she
said as she marveled at the excitement in his face.

"Maybe I should at that," he said as an idea was
obviously conceived and registered in the light of his
eyes. "Who's going with you on this?"

"Would you believe no one?" she said a little
bleakly. "I'm going to have to do the camerawork on
this, too, and make it sort of a travel documentary
pointing out the high spots from Fayetteville to Eureka Springs and down Highway Seven. I'd been pes-
tering Jim about more responsibility, and this is what I
got."

"Well, you've got someone with you now," he said
firmly. "I wouldn't miss this for the world."

"Are you crazy?" she asked. "You don't know anything about—"

"You can teach me," he said, cutting her off. "You
did it once. So you can do it again."

"I don't know about this," she said as the ramifica-

promised to fulfill so many of his idealistic dreams was
simply not there.

"You don't have the right to say something like
that," he said acidly. "Only someone who has had my
experience and the feelings it created within me could
make such a judgment."

Clay's disappointment hung heavy in the air. Instantly contrite, Jessica realized she had spoken without thinking and once again spears of dread snaked
through her as she saw something special flying away.
"I'm sorry, Clay," she said as she reached out to touch
his arm. "That was a terribly insensitive thing to say.
Of course I can understand your wanting to erase
emotions such as that."

He looked straight ahead as he drove the truck
through the silent night. He didn't want to forgive her
that easily. He had expected her of all people to understand.

"Please, Clay," said Jessica. "Let's not spoil our
ride. Remember what you just said back at the
house?"

He looked at her quizzically.

"You know, about forgiving and understanding?"

He slowed the truck as he gave her a careful look.
"Did I say that?" he asked as he pulled to the curb
and felt himself softening to her appeal, which was
frankly irresistible.

"Yes, you did," said Jessica as her eyes gleamed in
the dark in a shining plea and she thought of how
easily she seemed to go from one mess to another with
this man.

"Well, you know to begin with, I don't really live up
there all the time," he said a little petulantly. "I mean,

I'm not the only person in the world who has a retreat."

"That's right," said Jessica as she grabbed at the opportunity to end this. "You told me that. And, didn't we agree we'd both give the other's way of life a chance?"

"Yes, we did," he said as a little grin began to loosen him up. "You know, after all of this bickering tonight, we ought to be able to survive anything." He reached out and pulled her close. "Just don't ever think that way about me again," he said. "I really can't stand it."

"You owe me a banana split," she said as she pulled away from him laughingly after giving him a light kiss on the cheek. "You'd better be a man of your word if that's so important to you."

"Spoilsport," he said as he reluctantly released her breast from the cradle of his hand. But again he was impressed with her adroit use of humor in sticky situations and he knew this woman with all of her frailties and vulnerabilities as well as her gutsy bravado had to become a permanent part of his life.

"And I don't want a frozen custard stand either," she said. "It's Shuler's Ice Cream Parlor, or nothing," she added.

"Demanding woman to the end," he said. "She's even picky about her ice cream."

"My men too," she said coyly as a sudden rush of feelings went through her while she luxuriated in his physical aura and the sound of the humor in his voice. There was an underlying sexiness to it that instantly and simply drove her wild.

They drove in companionable silence to the town's best ice cream emporium, which served elaborate con-

coctions and charged prices to match. "S about your work and this special assi have," said Clay as they both labored o banana splits.

"Well, since you do business with the sta you know what a TV news reporter does. him a bit of an exasperated look.

"Well, pardon me," he said in sly exagge was just trying to be nice, since you've alread tonight I haven't shown any interest in wha Actually I got my start in TV way back w tiny local station where all they had were t floor cameras. I was an operator."

"Why, you fink," said Jessica in real outra "You acted like you didn't know a thing ab VCR equipment yesterday."

"I didn't," he said honestly. "That was years and years ago and today's equipment is a whole new ball game. And that modern portable stuff you carry all over the place must be something."

"Not if you've got a good cameraman as your partner," she said. "I really just love what I'm doing. A lot of it is humdrum, but every once in a while something really exciting comes along. I love investigative report ing and exposés."

"You would," he said with a grin. "I bet nothin gets past you when you're hot onto something."

"I hope not," she said fervently as she met his eye and marveled at how much she was enjoying th warm sharing of her interests and the camaraderie naturally created.

"So what's this assignment you're going on t morrow?"

tions of such a thing were immediately evident. Yet something in her also rejoiced at the thought of sharing such an experience with him. "Do you really think it would be all right?" she asked.

"Of course," he said. "Just leave it to me. Remember, I'm one of the station's best customers."

"Ah-ha!" she said with a contrived menace. "So you're not above throwing your weight around now and then when there is something you want to do."

"I never said I was," he said as he dodged her laughing barbs.

"So what happened to all of that morality?"

"Right where it belongs," he said adroitly. "I'm just offering a helping hand to a friend, and in any event this sounds like a perfect public relations setup to me. I'm sure the antique Cresent Hotel in Eureka Springs wouldn't turn down a little free publicity."

"Now, just hold on," said Jessica. "This is my story and my assignment!"

He couldn't restrain his laughter. "By all means," he said as he openly enjoyed the fiery sparks in her eyes and knew she was at her most attractive when she was in one of these fits of temper. "Are we going to take a book along so we'll know how to operate the camera?"

"You'll eat those words," she said as laughter lit up her eyes and enhanced all of her attractive features. "You'll be sorry you ever said them!"

"I wouldn't do anything to compromise your assignment," he said lovingly. "I was just looking for a business justification too—force of habit you know, but then who needs that. I'm free to do whatever I please."

"You sure seem to know all about these things though," said Jessica.

"What things?"

"Area attractions, that sort of thing."

"I guess so," he said. "Before I got so involved with my existence at Owl Hill I spent a great deal of time traveling. Odd, I hadn't missed it once in the past few years, but now all of a sudden it seems like it might be fun again."

"And who's going to take care of the animals?" asked Jessica as she suddenly wondered how all of the logistics of this wild scheme could possibly be worked out.

"Good point," he said. "Fortunately Bessie has gone dry so she won't need to be milked. The rest is no problem. I've had to spend several days away in the past, so I worked out a system to cover this."

"Is there nothing that you can't run by remote control?" asked Jessica incredulously.

"Yes," he said as a big grin broke out on his face. "My love life. I can't stand being away from you and we're going to have to do something about it."

"Such as?" she asked mischievously.

"Such as getting out of here and going back to your house, where I intend to make mad passionate love to you."

"Clay, for heaven's sake," she said in genuine shock, in spite of the fact that he was obviously teasing. "People can hear you."

"I don't care," he said, laughing. "That is really how I feel and that's what I want."

"And what about what *I* want?" she said half seriously. But it was no use. He was irresistible and she found herself responding to the very suggestion of making love with him in a wild outrageous way as waves of desire rolled over her and radiated from her eyes.

"That's what you want too," he said knowingly as he reached for her hand and pulled her into a loose embrace.

Their thighs touched, sending a warm shock up their bodies, and Jessica was glad they were in a remote corner booth. From the moment Clay had sat down next to her, Jessica had known his proximity would lead to a moment like this. They finished their ice cream like giggling school kids and then left arm in arm after Clay paid the bill.

A few moments later they were driving happily toward Jessica's house. When they arrived, they climbed the steps of her porch and suddenly Jessica was shy again. Clay immediately sensed it and pulled her close as the moon played down on their faces through a nearby trellis with a climbing rosebush on it. Enveloped in the heady perfume of the flowers, Clay tipped her chin up and gently kissed her and restrained his own impulse to crush her to him in a wild moment of possession, preferring instead to build to a mutual plateau of passion. Taking her hand, he walked over to a wooden porch swing and pulled her gently down into his lap and then settled into its creaky confines. "I used to do this with my best girls too," he murmured as he kissed her again and held her closer for some old-fashioned necking.

Jessica responded in warm abandon, grateful again for the perceptiveness of this man and his gentle ways. Yet there was a very real insistence about him, too,

111

and suddenly she just wasn't sure she could actually make love to him in her own home, the home she shared with Janey and had shared with Frank. But as his lips moved lower and the evening's balmy summer breezes blew around them, all of Jessica's senses responded in yet a new and delightful way, leaving her no alternative but to take advantage of such a wonderful opportunity.

In slow pantomime they moved into the house and Clay led her on insistently. "I need you," he said. But suddenly, as her paranoia touched him, it was his turn to be shy. He looked at her a bit hesitantly. "Somehow, though, I think maybe I shouldn't take advantage of this situation."

But in spite of his hesitancy his words were gauged with a hint of calculation and his breathing was heavy. Jessica pulled away, honestly impressed with his sensitivity. "Not on your life," she said in a low voice as suddenly she had no doubt about her own desires. "I've been dreaming of this moment all day."

The words were lost as he swept her into an embrace, crushing her lips to his in a ravaging wild intensity that left them both with no alternative other than to fulfill the destiny of the moment. Their bodies were already in a wild ecstatic delirium as they pushed the door of the bedroom aside and moved in perfect physical chorus toward the waiting bed. In seconds they were helping each other to pull away the constricting clothes as Clay buried his face in Jessica's breasts and began a wild dance of sensation over her body with his fingers. They trailed over her skin, raising tiny hackles of demanding passion from the soft down on her body and bringing it to bristling life in wild anticipation.

In a haze warm with Clay's masculine scent, Jessica buried her face in his hair, gasping to possess the very essence of him as once again he moved above her and their lips met in fiery parrying need. Pulling him closer, she reveled in his strength when she felt the length of his body on hers and responded to the tips of his fingers as they moved insistently over her body in perfect unison with his succoring lips until finally they found their quest in her dark triangle of silky down. Her body turned to molten liquid as rays of sensation flowed through her in answer to his magical massage.

Wantonly she moved to be more receptive, guiding the strength of his manhood to her in a suggestive, insistent way, while performing her own brand of exquisite titillation. Gasping, he no longer could control the forcefulness of his desire as he sought out the glistening softness she offered and plunged deeply, pulling her hips to him in a convulsive possessive way as he swiveled deeper and deeper, trying to find the very core of her creation. In wild response Jessica rose to meet him thrust for thrust as he continued in frenzied need.

Delirious with sensation, Jessica felt an out-of-body headiness as wave after molten wave promised to take her beyond anything she had ever experienced. When she peaked from his sweet ministrations, wild, titillating alarms were set off throughout her body, grasping him softly in the ultimate ecstasy. Then he pulled her higher and closer until he finally felt the charge of his strength leaving his body for a wild warm welcome in her own. In sweet gasping serenity he fell to his knees and lowered her gently to the bed before he happily covered her with his own spent body. In soft, lov-

113

ing caresses he moved his lips over her neck and brow and then reached down to once again kiss the breasts he loved so much. Moaning in contentment, Jessica allowed her hands to wander over him as endearments poured forth in answer to his own. Pushing his hair back from his brow, Jessica looked into his dark eyes and gave thanks for the moonlight that outlined the handsome, angled planes of his face and told her everything she wanted to know. "I love you," she said simply. "I don't know why or how, but I know I do."

His eyes crinkled in unbelievable joy as he pulled her close. "And I love you too," he whispered. "I've never been more sure of anything in my life."

Their eyes were locked in mutual agreement as he reached out to trace her ear and she responded with a nibble to his hand. "Stay with me," she said as the reality of the situation suddenly began to intrude.

"I never intended to leave," he said with a smile. "If I have my way, we'll never be apart again."

"That would be nice, wouldn't it?" she said with a smile, "but we have to remember Janey."

"I know," he said. "But I'm sure we can work this out in a sensible way."

"I think so," she said with a happy little yawn. "But that's the key word. We have to be sensible."

"Just lead me on," he said. "I'll do whatever you want to do."

"Does that include leaving Owl Hill?" An impertinent little smile rippled up from her lips to her eyes.

"Ah-ha," he said as he rose above her in mock hauteur. "Old basic human nature is always there to muck everything up. Surely you're endowed with some sense of fair play?"

114

"Maybe, maybe not," she said, clearly enjoying herself. "I guess it all depends on what your priorities are."

"If it's really that important to you," he said suddenly somber in a clearly mocking way, "and, obviously, speaking in this great moment of weakness, you know I'd do anything before I'd miss out on another romp like the one we just had."

"You cad," she said in sudden energetic response. "Spoken like a true male who has gotten what he wants. What makes you think I'd ever ask anyone I cared about to give up something that was so important to him? I thought I was going to spend some time with you up there."

"I'm not arguing," he said, laughing. "You're the one intent on causing trouble."

"Not me," she said huskily as she lay down beside him again. "All I want is to be with you, happy and content."

"This is content," he said jokingly. "Arguing with me and making half-hearted threats and demands two minutes after I've given you my very soul—"

"That's right," she said, smiling in her most coy way. "Sounds perfect to me."

115

CHAPTER SIX

Within an hour, though, as Clay lay beside her sleeping peacefully, the ugly talons of doubt and insecurity had once again begun to claw at Jessica. As she tossed restlessly she suddenly began to dwell on Janey, and even though the child wasn't there, Jessica couldn't deny the guilt as she wondered at her behavior in the house she shared with her child. Somehow it just wasn't right. In startling insight she realized she was, after all, a simple, old-fashioned girl and she couldn't face Janey in a situation such as this unless the bonds of marriage had legitimized it.

Yet there was something in her that also hesitated at that thought. Old-fashioned common sense told her she needed to know a great deal more about this man whom she simply couldn't resist before taking such an important and lasting step. She sighed and flung the sheet back. At the same time there was no way in the world she could deny the glory and ecstasy she had just shared with Clay. And she loved him sincerely

116

and deeply. She couldn't deny that. It was just that something about the timing and seeming impropriety of it nagged at her.

Getting up carefully, she pulled on a silk robe and headed for her living room. Feeling a need to somehow assuage the inexplicable guilt she felt when she thought of Janey, she shoved in the video cassette from the network baseball game she had recorded earlier. Maybe if she picked up some more pointers and really got herself ready for Janey's upcoming game . . .

As she turned it down low she headed for the refrigerator for a snack while the preliminary chatter from the announcers came on, giving statistics and other tidbits of baseball gossip, which she was finding a bit fascinating. Armed with a sandwich and milk, all of which somehow made her feel better, too, Jessica was soon comfortably ensconced in the deep, oversize couch avidly watching a hot game between the Royals and the Yankees. It wasn't long before she was unconsciously offering her vocal opinions and coaching instructions with reference to the pitchers and batters. When a base hit flew out and hit the wall she whooped in abandon because it had been made by the team she had unwittingly chosen as her favorite.

Clay came to the door groggily. "What in God's name are you up to now?" he asked as he tried to fathom exactly what was going on. "Do you know it's one in the morning?"

"Yes," Jessica said absently. "I just couldn't sleep, so I thought I'd do my homework for Janey."

"I don't believe you," he said as he came fully

awake. "You won't allow yourself one moment of peace, will you?"

"Oh, don't lecture me now," she said as she took a big bite of her sandwich. "Watch with me and tell me a little more about what's going on."

Incredulity wouldn't suffice as a description of his feelings, but as Clay looked at Jessica and at the little-girl look of interest and expectation that filled her face, he once again gave in to his soft, protective feelings and admitted how desperately he wanted to please her. "Looks like you've already watched a few games before tonight," he said as he listened to her cursing out the runner she had just been raving about a second before. "And your loyalty seems a bit fickle too."

"He's screwing up," she said excitedly. "If he tries to steal, they'll put him out, and they need that run."

"He's doing only what his coaches are telling him to do," said Clay, laughing.

"I don't care," she said. "It's a dumb thing to do."

"My, my, aren't we the expert," he said as he sat down beside her. "One book and a couple of games on TV and you've licked it, haven't you?"

"That's right," she said as the runner was called out just as she had predicted. "I knew he wasn't fast enough."

Clay looked at her in true perplexity. Was she really as charmingly ding-dong as she seemed to be at times or simply a truly perceptive rare talent? "You know, I think this is going to be very interesting," he said. "I'm not going to rest now until I get you to a major league game."

"In time," she said as she suddenly remembered what had driven her to this activity in the first place.

"Let's get the trip we have planned out of the way first and then think about that. You know I have to think of—"

"Janey, I know," he finished for her, nodding his head. "It's not going to be a problem," he said firmly as he turned her toward him and made her look at him. "Really, it isn't."

She looked at him a little sheepishly and then squirmed as she felt the now familiar warmness his nearness and touch always brought. As their minds synchronized on their intimate moments together only a few hours before, she felt safe again, and she reached out for his hand.

"You're probably right," she said. "But I've never had to handle anything like this before."

"We'll handle it together," he said as he reached to pull her closer. Their lips came together in a sweet caress and Jessica felt the wild onslaught of her responses both physical and emotional. In sweet ecstasy she reached up to trace the handsome angles of his face and then settled happily into his arms as the action of the field suddenly broke loose. It effectively broke the mood as Jessica whooped again and had an absolute fit over a home run. "Oh, well," said Clay as he smoothed his sleep-tousled hair and sat back to watch the rest of the game. "It was a nice thought."

Nevertheless, when they returned to bed a while later they snuggled sleepily into each other's arms and settled in softly as their bodies molded together in a totally natural way. Clay's lips brushed the nape of her neck one last time as he murmured, "Good night, sweetheart," and Jessica finally drifted away in very contented slumber.

The next morning was a bit hectic as Clay explained his interest in the trip to Jim Reynolds and then they awkwardly loaded all of the equipment they would need. "Isn't it a little strange that you know all about being a cameraman as well as a reporter?" he asked. He was a little breathless as they tossed the last of the load into Jessica's little car.

"Not really," she said as she checked to see if everything was packed securely. "I figured if I was going to have a career in communications I should learn about everything, and it's one of the reasons why I was hired, because I could do both."

"Figures," he said with a hint of a smirk, his blue eyes ever mischievous. "You'd never be satisfied with just one specialty."

"Not really," she said as she dusted her clothes and prepared to get into the car. "Actually it's just a part of the overall communications curriculum I completed at the vocational school. I love reporting, but I liked the technical side of it too. Now I have the option of being a director, which is strictly technical stuff in TV, or a producer, the person who actually puts the whole show together and runs it."

"Sounds like another bout of Superwoman to me," he said teasingly as he slid in beside her and savored the hint of a pugnacious set to her jaw as the car motor roared to life.

"Not at all," she said as she began to back up. "That's what I call being smart and covering all of your bases."

"Oh, boy," he said as he marveled at her quick unconscious conversion to baseball lingo. "Remind me to do something—"

"What?" she asked absently as they pulled out into traffic and headed for Highway Seven.

"Never to buy you an encyclopedia. I don't think I could stand to live with someone who is a certified expert on everything."

"You wish," she said spiritedly. But a smile nevertheless played around her lips as she looked into his laughing eyes accented by a nonchalant lock of hair that insisted upon falling awry. "I only wish I did know everything so I'd never have to worry about anything again."

"You'd be bored to tears in five minutes," he said as he reached out to give her an affectionate nudge and instantly responded to the fire the warmth of her skin always ignited. "Of course I'd do my best to keep things interesting for you in . . . other ways," he said huskily as she assiduously tried to look straight ahead, a victim of the intimate circumstances herself. "Wonder where I could read up on the topic. . . ."

"You need lessons in that?" she asked drolly.

"Only if you think so," he said, laughing.

"Hmm," she said coyly. "I may need to think that over."

He was more than equal to her facetious comments as the rugged planes of his face mirrored his delight. "Does that mean I'll get to audition again?"

She laughed outrageously. The sparks between them were mutual and natural as this sensuous repartee continued while they drove on out to Owl Hill. Clay quickly gathered together his necessities for the trip and made sure everything was secure for the next few days. The camaraderie between them was perfect and pleasant as Clay continued to joke and looked longingly toward his bedroom. But Jessica hurried him along as she pointed out the time. She had to accomplish a lot over the next few days, and her strong professional drive was now in strong contention with her physical responses. The mood continued happy, though, until suddenly Clay stopped the car with a jerk.

"What's the matter?" asked Jessica, alarmed.

"Damn it to hell," he said, suddenly very angry. "Someone's been out here on the edge of my property again. I'm telling you, when I get back I'm going to install some monitor cameras and do something to get this stopped."

"Clay, for heaven's sake," said Jessica, alarmed now. "This is national forest around here."

"I don't care," he said, but already his ire was diminishing as he saw the stricken look on her face and realized that he was overreacting foolishly. He glanced at her again as they started to move and gave her a sheepish little grimace. "I can't help the feelings I have about this place."

The silence hung between them for several seconds as Jessica swallowed and reached out to touch him. "You know, someone said, 'To rely on yourself is to be a warrior in a contemporary society, but you don't need to be armed with a gun, just excellence.' "

He looked at her, a bit astounded, as the wisdom of the words immediately washed over him and tinged his response with a laughing derisiveness. "Don't tell me," he said. "You got that from some damn book too!"

"You bet," she said as her body relaxed in relief. But the easiness of their earlier mood was lost as Clay

122

drove rapidly with a hint of vengeance over the twisting mountain highway known for its scenic beauty.

Before long Jessica was beginning to feel the effects as her stomach began to churn in a queasy way. She readily recognized it as a combination of both stress and motion. And although Clay had seemingly returned to his earlier cheerful self, she was still tense over his outburst. She grew quieter and quieter as she tried to mentally and physically quell her reactions.

They were just outside Eureka Springs when she knew they were going to have to stop. Clay immediately responded as a steep drive coming down to a curve in the road loomed ahead of them. "Here, this is a perfect spot," he said as he pulled to the side of the road.

Seeing her pallor, he rapidly helped her from the car and began to walk with her up the graveled lane. A scenic sign pointed the way to Thorncrown Chapel. Almost miraculously, as the cool breeze from the surrounding pine forest blew over her and she nestled into the steadiness of his arms, Jessica felt better immediately. As they topped the hill they had been climbing, both were astounded and enchanted by the beauty of the towering chapel, which was a narrow modern sculpture of rugged poles and glass nestled in and among and over the trees. The sun glancing from the huge windows was like a splatter of jewels in the wilderness, and they unconsciously clasped hands as they walked on toward it.

In the hushed stillness of the scene Clay looked at her again and solicitously appraised her appearance and demeanor as she turned with shining eyes to respond, clearly overwhelmed by the enchantment of the place. "Feeling better?" he asked.

"Yes," she said. "I guess I just needed to get out of the car."

"Well, why didn't you tell me sooner?" he asked.

"We were almost to Eureka Springs and I guess I just hate to think of being such a bother."

He looked at her a bit impatiently and then as the ambience of the scene magnified all of his usual care and concern a million times over he turned her around gently. "Munchkin," he said as he led her to a bench where they could sit down. "When was the last time you honestly thought about just you? Nobody else or anything else, just you?"

She looked at him a little strangely, not prepared for this sudden intimate turn in the conversation, and then also in accord with the nature of the setting answered him honestly. "I guess when we were together making love," she said softly. "Nothing else matters then." Unconsciously she reached out to touch the bronze planes of his face and shuffled her feet before she turned away in embarrassed confusion.

"And then five minutes later you're feeling guilty as hell," he said. A hint of impatience had entered his voice again and his blue eyes pierced straight through her. "We're going to have to stop it."

She snapped her head back and looked at him a bit anxiously. "Stop w-what?" she stammered.

"Feeling guilty," he said as he raised her chin and reached down to kiss her.

In the stillness of the forest around them everything seemed to stop and Jessica knew she had another moment to savor for the rest of her life. She moved into his arms and luxuriated in the wealth of his warm embrace. "Let's go inside," he said as his breath whispered through her hair, "and talk to the Man. I think it's time to make this relationship legal."

"What do you m-mean?" stammered Jessica, just a bit panicked in spite of her rampaging emotions.

"I mean, I think we should get married and this looks like the perfect place to do it."

"Oh, not without Janey and my family being a part of it," cried Jessica. "I mean, I love you and I think that's what I want, that is, if you're asking me," she added with a hint of her usual spirit.

He smiled in spite of himself. She was going to be a handful, no doubt about it.

"But," she went on as she leaned back and held tightly to his wide shoulders as she looked into his eyes, "when we do it I want Janey to see that there is some formality to the whole thing before she wakes up and finds a man has moved in with her mother. I mean, it won't be long and she'll be having ideas herself. I can't very well say, 'Do as I say, but not as I do.' "

He loved her even more then as his heart reached out to hers. He couldn't dispute her inborn morality that seemed to consider everyone who surrounded her. "Well, I can understand that and respect it," he said softly. "It's just that I don't want to see you suffer because you're experiencing honest emotions and reactions with me that make us both very happy."

He looked around and the beauty of the place seemed to inspire him. "Come with me," he said. He took her hand and they walked up to the chapel. He pushed the heavy doors open and they walked in bathed in streaming sunlight. Clay moved toward the altar with Jessica in tow, somewhat in awe of the whole experience. "In this place, before man and God, I thee wed," he said as he reached for her hand and brought it to his lips.

Tears sprang to Jessica's eyes as feelings beyond description washed over her.

"That's how I feel and that's the promise I'm making to you now," he said as he stood before her tall and humble, his eyes never leaving hers. "We'll do all of the formal legal things just as soon as you want, but in my heart and mind I'm already married to you, bound to you for life."

"And I to you," said Jessica sincerely as the peace and holiness of the place gave her courage. "From this moment on we are one together in body and soul, and I'll love you always."

Their lips came together in a sweet communion that lifted them beyond the confines of the ethereal structure and bound them in an irrevocable promise.

"Till death us do part," said Clay huskily as they turned to leave, and Jessica snuggled happily in his one-arm embrace that seemed to bind her to him permanently.

When they came out the sun was warm and the whole world was a vivid green. Summer aromas of sweet outdoors washed over them and Jessica knew she had never been so happy or content in her life. This was her moment, hers alone to share with Clay, and for the first time that truly seemed to be perfectly all right. She felt secure and happy and knew she would never have to worry about anything again because Clay would take care of everything. It was a shed her hair back. "I just . . . I can't ex-

moment he almost thought it was hopeless,
his common sense and understanding came to
e. They had moved very fast to this moment.
e at the chapel was almost a dream. But now
d that all of Jessica's original hesitancy had
. It was almost uncanny. He could see it when
d not.

se fleeting seconds while Jessica tried to iden-
emotions and the reactions that accompanied
e remembered all of the events that had tran-
in these few days. The campground and the
ve emotions they had experienced together. His
latile reaction when he had learned about her
yesterday, and his disappointment about her
g impatience over his convictions, all of which
e unimportant when they thought about the
line—how much they obviously needed each
It was a simple matter of trust and understand-
hey had to have that before they could have the
they both coveted most—security and faith in
destined happiness.

h an infinite patience and wisdom he didn't
he possessed, he went to her. "Jess," he said
, "come back to me. I know what's happening."
e turned to him and understood immediately. As
eelings they had shared at the chapel washed over
gain she returned to his arms. "Oh, Clay," she
"I just don't want to make any mistakes. I can't
the thought of my being just an easy fling to you,
want you and I need you so much."

feeling she had first experienced at the ill-fated campground and now she honestly enjoyed it.

"Now, what do you say to a short honeymoon in
the Crescent Hotel, where Teddy Roosevelt once
stayed," said Clay as they ambled to the car in perfect
happy accord. "And Eureka Springs is just the place
to fix up what ails you." There was mischief in his
voice again. "I'll take you down to the Palace Hotel
and give you a hot mineral bath, but I'll take care of
the massage if you don't mind."

"Sounds like you had all of this planned," teased
Jessica, suddenly her usual piquant self again.

"Might have," he said, grinning. "If I didn't, I
should have."

"Well, you know what a pushover I am for a bath,"
she said, laughing, as her thoughts returned to their
first meeting and they both remembered that cold, wet
morning at the campground. It seemed like a reminis-
cence more appropriate for a golden wedding anniver-
sary, when in reality it was little more than a week
ago. There was simply no denying that they were old
souls meeting once again in a final, happy, destined
way, and they were both glowing from their mutual
meeting of mind and spirit as Clay handed her back
into the car.

"Do you think we should shoot some footage of this
place?" he asked.

"Sure," she said as a story quickly formed in her
mind and she knew exactly what she wanted to say
about it. "Let's get some snapshots too. I think I'm
going to want to remember this place in every way
possible for the rest of my life."

The look on his face was a memory in itself and

Jessica wondered if there was a limit to the heights she could experience with this man. When they left a while later, laughing and joking after their first mutual attempt with the professional video equipment, they were happy and content. It seemed a logical extension of the dream they were living when they pulled up to the antique entrance of the Crescent Hotel a half hour later.

Jessica looked around at the surrey in the yard, the wide concrete porch, and the etched-glass windows on the tall double wooden doors. Everything was exactly as it had been when the hotel was at its height as a modern Victorian establishment.

"Come on," said Clay as he enjoyed her reaction. "It gets better."

Jessica followed him, compelled by both personal and professional forces as her reporter's antennae made their invisible presence known. This was wonderful. The whole trip was going to be one of the best things she had ever done. Not only because of the uniqueness of the area, but also because just being around Clay made her feel more alive, more aware of her surroundings, simply happy to be alive.

The lobby and restaurants lived up to their antique promise and moments later they were comfortably settled in a bright, spacious room. Tenderly Clay turned her toward him and kissed her gently. "I've never been so happy," he said.

"Nor I," she answered as she responded to his caress. "But we need to get going. There's so much to see around here."

"First things first," he said as his voice dropped. "Right now I need to know how much you love me."

128

His lips and hands had a
and Jessica couldn't resist. I
to fulfill the emotions they ha
chapel. In a timeworn way th
ral desires as they dropped to
of sensation. Happily and h
wanting only the heat of the
warm friction that left them de
As Clay's lips caressed her bro
fire over her body, Jessica once
supreme out-of-body experienc
duced in such an exquisite way.
ous instant Jessica was sudden
guilt and doubt that left her imi

"I need to know how much y
an echoing taunt. In an instant
Jessica suddenly wondered abou
tive morality she was practicing.
man, yet every time she turned ar
into his arms in passionate need
carnal demands. Only moments be
in a holy place making solemn pro
a dream, crazy and nonsensical. T
she was constantly giving herself to
the flimsiest of promises totally un
common-sense facts.

Perceptive as always, Clay immed
as her body stiffened. "I thought w
this," he said as she turned away fr
shakily from the bed.

She looked at him and felt enormou
mixed in with a yearning and confu
couldn't understand. "I—I thought s

129

"That's why I think we should get married now," he said.

"But that's not right either," she said. "We've been over that. It's too soon, Clay and as much as we feel for each other, I think we have a lot to settle between us before we make that kind of commitment."

"I know," he said as he ran his hands through her hair and caressed her brow. "Then we've got to trust each other and understand what we're talking about when we say that."

"But you see," said Jessica, suddenly as intuitive as he. "That's the whole thing. You've already told me you don't trust anyone and I trust everyone. How do we know what we're doing? Somehow it just gets down to this wild physical thing and I know in the end there's got to be more than that."

"There is more than that," he said as he held her away from him and appealed to her to believe him. "You've given something to me that's fresh and fine. All of a sudden I can believe again and I don't ever want to lose that feeling."

"But that might have happened with anyone. You've isolated yourself for so long. . . ." Her face reflected her anguish.

"It was meant to happen with you," he said firmly. "I'll never believe anything else. You said you love me and I love you. That's what we have to believe in and trust."

"It's not very realistic," she said.

"It's what all of history has depended upon," he answered, "and we just made sacred promises to each other. I can't give you any more than that, but until you're absolutely sure, I'll do whatever you want. If

131

you want me to sleep in another room, I'll do it. If you want me to—"

The look on her face was an almost instant comical relief. "Oh, no," she cried. "You see, that's the whole thing. I can't bear the thought now of not being with you, but some little evil thing in me keeps saying it won't last, but go on and enjoy it anyway. That's what seems so wrong." Her words slowed as the realization they brought washed over her. Then her face was a bright picture of happiness. "That's it, isn't it?" she cried. "I just can't believe that something so great is happening to me and it's all right!"

"I think so," he said in like jubilation. "It's just a question of honestly believing this is happening to us."

"Is it?" she asked with just the last trace of tentativeness.

"It is," he said as he stood tall, putting all of the strength of his big frame behind his words. "And when you're ready, we're going to go back to that chapel and make it final before everyone you think is important. But as far as I'm concerned, it's final already. Now all you have to do is accept it."

Tears came to her eyes as the last doubt washed away. "I accept," she said. "And I also promise that there will never be any secrets or deceptions."

"No secrets," he said as he kissed her lightly. "And we share everything."

"Does that mean I can show the tapes of Owl Hill to the Brownies?" she said, suddenly mischievous as her usual happy spirits returned.

"I guess so," he said, pleased with the change in her demeanor. "That is, if I'm not too 'silly' in it."

"You're not. It's wonderful." She paused then as she

considered once again reiterating exactly how she had originally conceived that idea and then decided to leave it alone. Clay had already said he understood.

He looked at her as the panorama of her thoughts played over her face and never in his life had felt such tender desire. Her eyes were shining and happy, making her exceptionally beautiful, and he wanted every part of her to be a part of him. "You know," he said softly as he reached out to her again. "I want you very much right now, but because I love you I think this is the time to just say that and let you go. Maybe what we're really missing is the chance we didn't have to know each other as friends before we became lovers and because of that we've sort of missed out on the nuts and bolts of the bond it would have created."

"I think you're right," she said shyly as she reached out to him at the same time with an affectionate gesture. "I guess when you're as crazy as we are for each other the groundwork is somehow left out."

"So here's to being friendly," he said in a sudden exaggerated mock toast as he twirled her around in happy abandon and caught her hands.

"How friendly are you talking about?" she asked as her body began to instantly warm to his and her face mirrored a tinge of doubt.

"As friendly as you want to be," he shouted as he pulled her close and whirled her around in his arms after lifting her bodily from the floor. "I couldn't ever give up kissing you and holding you," he said as he set her down and fell breathlessly onto the bed. "Just come over here and stay close to me for a few more minutes and then we'll go out and see this town and learn everything we need to know about each other so there won't be any problems with loving each other tonight."

"You're impossible," she said as she laughed again and crawled happily into his arms, reveling in his strength and the feeling of security his gentle embrace gave to her. As he kissed her lightly and cautiously they both knew there was no denying the physical bond that had been there almost from the beginning. But it was also good to know that the restraint and concern he had displayed from the time of their very first intimate encounter was a consistent part of his character. Jessica smiled and felt its warmth radiate inwardly throughout her body. She knew now she could be happy with this man and there was no need to hurry. They had just promised each other that it would last forever.

CHAPTER SEVEN

The next few months were nearly idyllic for Clay and Jessica. They finished her news assignment and discovered that not only were they compatible as both friends and lovers, they were also a good media team. It was as if they were linked together into a perfect strong chain. They had capped their trip with the visit to Mary Maestri's in tiny Tonitown and Jessica was still exclaiming over it.

"There it was," she'd tell everyone, "out in the middle of this big field on Highways One-twelve and Sixty-eight. This beautiful big white building, elegant and classy that could almost have been a church. . . ."

The food was fantastic and she would never forget gazing at Clay through candlelight in the sumptuous interior while they giggled over the fantastically low prices and noted all the celebrities who had been there and left some memento that could be hung on the wall.

135

"It just goes to prove," Clay had said as they enjoyed the rich spumoni ice cream topped with a special liqueur. "It's just what you said."

"What are you talking about?" she had asked as she reveled in the warmth of the liqueur with the cold spumoni.

"When you said excellence is all that you need . . ."

"Oh, that," she said. But as the memory of those words came back to her she also remembered what had prompted them and hoped their newfound understanding of each other would also result in Clay's being a little less paranoid about his sanctuary at Owl Hill. She smiled, though, as she also remembered how they had shopped in the antique stores in Eureka Springs—walking up and down the narrow old streets, their arms filled with handmade dolls for Janey and a kit for a gigantic dollhouse Clay intended to build with her. Candles, books, and pottery, nearly all of it handmade by local artisans, had tempted them. The vanilla scent and Spencer Brewer piano music they had encountered in the cool confines of the Furry Company, an elegant art gallery, was still with her. *Surely after all of this he would begin to relax,* she thought.

She had another chance to make her point as they headed down a lonely highway toward home. They saw a roadside vegetable stand and pulled into a deserted farmer's yard. Although there was no one about, a jar had been placed in the center of the produce with a sign indicating the prices and instructions to leave payment in the jar. "You see," said Jessica as they were both struck with this demonstration of an old-fashioned honor system, "some people still trust strangers."

"Yeah, and it doesn't look like they're doing very well either," he said derisively with a hard set to his jaw. "I'll bet half of the people who stop here rip them off."

She had given him a terrible look as she dropped change for their purchases into the jar. But it was soon forgotten when they had visited the Civil War battlefield at Pea Ridge and became engrossed in the making of Jessica's documentary.

It seemed only natural that Jessica should take an honest interest in Clay's work. It wasn't long before she was involved with some of his projects, and true to his word he finally took her to a big league baseball game after her interest in the sport had become practically insatiable. Clay laughed as she continued to work with the Brownies, getting them ready for that first big camping trip, always taking a portable battery-operated TV on their outings if a game was scheduled.

Jessica's excitement when they went to see the Royals in Kansas City while also taking care of some of Clay's business was almost limitless. Her enthusiasm, however, soon dampened as balls came whizzing into the stands. They had gone early and had a beer or two along with several hot dogs before the game began. Now Jessica was definitely anxious over their lack of protection as they sat just outside of the net behind home plate.

"We're going to be killed here," she said as two stodgy old gents who had obviously been coming to baseball games all of their lives tried to ignore her.

Clay laughed as he tried to calm her down. "You

137

should have brought your glove," he said jokingly. "Most of the fans love a chance to catch a ball."

"Forget that," she said derisively as another foul tip came whizzing in. "That thing was like a bullet."

Clay had barely opened his mouth to assure her that they were quite safe when a ball came flying in and beaned an older man squarely in the head. He sat just a few rows below them. Jessica was horror-stricken as a stretcher was brought in and the man was taken to a hospital. "That does it," she said as she also felt the dizzying effects of her last beer. "I can't tell what's going on here anyway. I need the TV announcers to clue me in." She squinted out toward the large scoreboard and then really looked puzzled. "I didn't know baseball teams had anything to do with the women's movement," she said.

Clay gave her an astounded look and then began to laugh as he saw what she was pointing to. "Earned Run Average," he said. "ERA is earned run average."

"Oh," she said in embarrassment as the old men in front of them shuffled but looked straight ahead. "Too much beer?"

"Maybe," he said affectionately, charmed by her condition more than affronted. "But then maybe it might help if you read the whole book before you became such an expert," he teased as he tousled her hair and pulled her close for a quick kiss.

Contrite now, she sat meekly through the rest of the game enjoying another beer and hot dog as the time stretched out and she decided she definitely liked watching the games from her comfortable couch on TV more than live in these hard stadium seats. Suddenly everyone around them began to move and stand up. "Is it over?" she asked, wondering how she had missed that.

"No," said Clay as he continued to humor her. "This is the seventh-inning stretch."

"Stretch?" she questioned. "I thought that was something in a horse race."

The two old men who were standing and massaging their tired bottoms couldn't resist turning to get a good look at her after that.

"I think I'd better take you home," said Clay as they both began to laugh. Later they laughed for hours as they relived the day and Jessica's mind was no longer clouded with the beer. And after that every time something really idiotic came between them they found an easy and humorous way out of it by simply referring to the ERA or the seventh-inning stretch.

The happiest occurrence was Jessica's honest love for Owl Hill and the way Clay lived there. But with her own enjoyment she more than ever felt that he should be capable of sharing his happy experience there, but his privacy was one thing he remained adamant about. To make Jessica comfortable he installed a small satellite dish that brought in eighty television stations, but at the same time, true to his word, he also installed monitor cameras at regular intervals on the perimeter of his property.

"Now that we're going in and out of here so much," he explained, "it's bound to be noticed even on these backwoods roads and I think we need this kind of security."

It sounded very logical, but Jessica nevertheless felt a certain sense of defeat over it. The bright side of it was Janey's reaction to the monitors. She thought the cameras were something straight out of a space movie and never failed to mug and do whatever she could to get herself on the recording tape when they were arriving or just out walking together. In mutual agreement, though, they still continued to keep Owl Hill's exact location somewhat of a secret.

In her typical fashion Jessica was soon involved with every conceivable pioneer project imaginable, which included planting special beds of marigolds to use as a natural dye for the wool they sheared from the sheep which she then, of course, planned to spin into wool. She was fascinated with the idea of knitting sweaters from yarn with such a unique history. Likewise she was soon into canning and antiques, dried herb wreaths, and every other imaginable project promoting self-sufficiency that might come to mind until Clay once again was trying to lovingly curb her excesses.

As they enjoyed the glory of the autumn months Clay continued to talk about marriage. Janey and everyone in their families seemed happy for them and obviously expected such a development. But somehow Jessica had developed a certain ambivalence about it. Once she had gotten her reactions under control and Janey was obviously suffering no ill effects from the relationship with Clay, Jessica was content with their arrangement. She had love and security sealed with a sacred promise, but was still supremely independent, free to pursue her career and other interests. Remembering the sting of her first marriage, and the subconscious constriction she had felt then, she was loath to make more of a commitment now. So she still played for time, using her most appealing wiles to accomplish it. Everything seemed to be meshing in a happy, hectic way. Since completing the documentary, her career had blossomed and she was becoming a bit of a local celebrity; and now with Clay's help she easily kept up with Janey's needs and interests.

Their time was almost evenly divided between town and Owl Hill, when suddenly all of Clay's initial paranoia about his privacy seemed to burst forth in a very ugly way. Hunting season had begun, and one of Clay's animals was somehow shot, apparently by an encroaching poacher. He was so outraged that he once again began to stay at Owl Hill all of the time. Jessica tried to talk with him, but he simply and firmly closed her out. He began to carry his gun again and went out on long forays, often coming home with a stubborn, determined look on his face. Jessica was totally bewildered, unable to understand how one incident could cause such a huge overreaction after all they had been through together.

"Clay, we've got to talk about this," she said for the hundredth time as she wrung her hands and finally insisted that they set it straight.

"Don't you know what this means?" he fumed. "My security has been invaded. I've taken every precaution and it wasn't enough."

"It is," she cried. "You can't let this affect you this way."

"It's not just me," he said. "Can't you see that now it's not even safe for campers around here? Someone is coming into this area who either doesn't know anything about hunting regulations or they're just looking for trouble. Until we find out who this is, it's not safe for you to be driving out here alone either."

"But hunting is allowed in the national forest, isn't it?" she asked.

"Only in designated areas," he said. "When you get a hunting license they tell you all of those things, so there's no excuse for this."

"Well, surely the rangers and game wardens will take care of this. It's probably only an isolated incident."

"I don't think so," he said gloomily. "All of my instincts tell me there is more to this."

"Well, what about my instincts?" she asked as her voice dropped to a throaty, intimate level. "After all we've shared together, is this any time to go back to your old reclusive paranoia? You promised me that we would share everything and be happy."

He looked at her and felt an honest exasperation. He could sense something strange, maybe dangerous about to take place, and he was frustrated in his efforts to find out what it was. His years out here had taught him to recognize such things, but this was so nebulous that he couldn't find sensible words to explain it. But now as he looked at Jessica, who never failed to appeal to him, he felt only an honest sense of protectiveness. He wanted to be happy and secure with her again. His inclination was to put her in a safe place and then prepare to aggressively handle this threat in whatever way was necessary to end it.

Jessica watched his face and perceptively saw the softening of his emotions. In the only way she knew how, she climbed into his arms in a now very familiar way and in seconds all either of them could think of was being together and loving each other as they had done so many times in the past. Clay's lips caressed her brow and endearments, all the sweeter because they were tinged with the honey of making up, swept them away in an ocean of physical passions that neither could deny.

"Don't pull away from me," breathed Jessica as her lips ruffled through his hair. "Sharing trouble is just as important as sharing the good things." She reveled in the strength of his hard body as he pulled her closer, and they basked in the warmth of the fire in the fireplace while he began to pull her garments away.

In a seeming need to fulfill both their mental and physical needs they continued to address the issue of their estrangement while their passion escalated as a fitting background of sure mediation.

"I want you to be safe," whispered Clay as he looked into her eyes and deliberately toyed with her breasts. "I can't bear the thought of you being hurt." He watched in satisfaction as her nipples grew hard and taut between his teasing fingers.

She reached eagerly to kiss him, pulling him close so she could feel the thatch of the hair on his chest near her bare skin. "But I don't want you out here alone thinking these strange morose thoughts," she sighed as she nibbled on his ears and moved her hands suggestively down his torso until she pulled away the last of his garments in a practiced movement, smiling as she heard him gasp in sweet satisfaction. "It was just an accident," she continued as she gloried in the strength of his ready desire and moved so his lips could suckle her aching breasts while his arms went around her and pulled her securely beneath his throbbing, probing body. "I can't bear to have anything come between us," she gasped as his lips came crushing down on hers and she felt the simultaneous parrying of both his tongue and fingers with the most intimate parts of her body.

She met his tongue thrust for thrust with her own as her body arched in wild response to his tender explorations and wave after wave of wild, hot desire spread from that sensitive area of response throughout her body.

"It's only until I know for sure what's going on out here," he insisted as he pinned her more securely beneath him and paused to look deeply into her eyes. "Then we'll get married," he said, "so there won't be any question about that ever again."

Jessica met his eyes and was so inflamed with the passion he had aroused as he continued to expertly bring her to the shattering peak she so desired that she nodded in numb assent. "Whatever you want," she said breathlessly as she opened her body and urged him to give her the ultimate fulfillment that only his body could bring as it delved to the bed of her creation with strong, forceful thrusts that touched her to her very soul.

In firm agreement, filled with an obvious satisfaction that she would listen and do as he wished, he rose above her and brought his pounding strength to her in motions that nevertheless were filled with a sweet cherishing urgency as he pulled her soft body close and they both gave in to a flurry of wordless nibbling caresses until at last their lips locked together in simultaneous grinding, parrying need in unison with the rest of their bodies. After moments of sheer wild, exquisite, driving anticipation they grasped each other in

"I can explain that to you," she said as she fully and totally realized what was going to happen and she had inadvertently flamed Jim's interest in Clay with her feeble attempt to protect him.

"I'll bet," he said as he turned his back in dismissal. "Go on out and pick up the garden club assignments. I need a real reporter for this job."

Her eyes were stinging with tears as she stumbled from the news director's office. She had often heard and been a part of the seemingly cold and dispassionate side of newsmaking with its incessant snooping and professional objectivity, but never had she believed that it could actually be more important than the feelings of another human being. In cold reality she realized that that was exactly the way it was. The only thing different now was that it was her feelings and Clay's that were being ignored. The news came first. Nothing else mattered. That was the universal creed, and when something became news, it must be reported no matter who might be hurt. She had believed that and conducted her reporting in that way, always thinking she had been fair and objective. Now she wondered as she walked gloomily over to the assignment desk.

Mike Carter, a new and extremely ambitious young reporter, brushed past her, and she saw him enter Jim Reynolds's office. Through the windows that partitioned it from the rest of the studio workroom she immediately understood what was going on. She looked at the papers in her hand and suddenly she knew she had to do something to stop this. She had no inclination to complete these boring assignments and

a final shuddering crescendo as if to truly meld their bodies into one.

For the next hour they kissed and loved each other with a soft, cherishing passion as both wanted the moment of closeness to last forever. It was as if both sensed, as if by mutual premonition, that these moments, with their sweet, universal bonding that both held precious, might, in spite of their fevered words just moments before, be coming to an end.

When Jessica returned to town the next morning with the understanding that she was not to come out to Owl Hill again until Clay gave the okay, her sense of doom was suddenly a reality she didn't want to face. The news was all over town that strange things were happening to campers out in the national forest area and suddenly the whole town had gotten wind of Clay's hideaway there and his rather eccentric lifestyle.

In absolute horror she listened when Jim Reynolds called her into his office. "Now, what was this you were telling me about last spring when you went out there camping? You've gotten pretty close to this guy Farley since then, haven't you?"

"Well, yes . . . yes," she stammered as she realized the nightmare she had originally anticipated after her ill-conceived idea to go out and tape Clay's complex was about to happen. "But this whole thing is ridiculous."

"Well, something is going on out there. People are getting shot at and having their camps torn up. Nobody's been hurt, but weird things happen in the night that scare the wits out of some of them, and you told me yourself this guy runs around with a gun chasing people from his property."

"That isn't what I s-said exactly," she stammered a bit lamely as she remembered her rather exaggerated presentation when she wanted to do that story. She could have killed herself now as she remembered how she had rationalized, saying it was for Clay's own good too. He needed to be a little more forthcoming. Now everything that he had feared could very easily happen and she knew what that would do to his attitude. Everything that they had accomplished together in such a happy and loving way would surely be lost. He would never trust her or anyone again, let alone want to have anything to do with her.

"I take it," said Jim in his usual gruff way, "you're saying you don't want anything to do with this assignment now."

"Assignment?" she said, aghast.

"That's right," he said. "This could be one of the biggest investigative exposés we've ever had around here. The papers haven't got wind of it yet other than to report an isolated incident or two on a back page. But with what you told me last spring, I see a real angle."

He watched her intently, but Jessica was having none of this. Never, never would she consent to be a part of something she knew was totally misguided. She opened her mouth to try to set him straight, but he cut her off. "The least you could do," he said, "since you obviously are no longer interested in being a first-rate reporter, is tell us where his place is and what goes on out there."

"Do you know what you're asking of me?" she said.

146

"Yes."

"I'd never do anything like that," she said voice rose an octave and her words were tinge anger. "I'm not just a casual acquaintance of thi I love him."

"Oh," said Jim knowingly as his voice took sudden songlike quality. "Then that means couldn't be objective about any of this anyway. might even cover up for him."

"There is nothing to cover up," she said v mently, "and I don't think you have a right to inv a man's privacy like this."

"Oh, a little change in your tune, I'd say. Th certainly not the way you looked at it last spring.'

"That was different then," she spat out.

"So it was," he said. He gave her another long lo and pursed his lips as he bounced back and forth for moment in his desk chair. "I think you know a whol lot more about this than what you're letting on. Bu now I couldn't trust anything you have to say anyway so I'm going to put someone on this who I know wil get to the bottom of it."

"I don't know any more about this than you do," she said. "You're really going in the wrong direction."

"Oh, yeah," he said as his feet dropped with a thump. "We've already learned about all of his big electronic and communications purchases. How many people buy big satellite dishes and monitoring cameras who live out in the woods? This man isn't some backwoods hermit. He's as sharp as they come, and I've been in the news business too long not to know when something funny is going on, especially when you put the facts together and two and two make four."

147

after this she wasn't sure if she really wanted to be a news reporter.

Without thinking, she dropped the slips of paper and walked out of the room. She went rapidly to her car and had only one thing in her mind. She had to get word to Clay and let him know what was going on. More importantly, she had to let him know she didn't have anything to do with this.

She went home and tried desperately to call him on his special telephone, but there was no answer. She remembered all of his recent treks with his gun and suddenly in a moment of doubt she wondered just what he had been doing during those times. She couldn't recall his ever having called the rangers or game warden, but then in absolute chagrin she pushed those terrible thoughts from her mind. How could she ever think such things? She knew Clay was a gentle and passionate man who would never hurt anyone unless he was threatened or someone violated his privacy.

With those last thoughts she went into a complete panic. She had to see Clay and get this all straight in her mind. Maybe Jim was right. She had lost her objectivity and now she wouldn't know the truth if it hit her in the face. After all, the entire relationship with Clay had been rather eccentric. But in her heart she knew there was a reasonable explanation for all of this and now she just had to keep her wits about her until this was completely cleared up.

She called her mother and rapidly made arrangements for Janey's care when the child returned from school and then hurried to her car. Jessica drove recklessly, fighting tears and hysteria half the way and then chastising herself into a quasi calm as first one devil's advocate and then another fought to possess her mind. She was just rounding a bend near a large rock mass in the national forest when suddenly the roar of a rock slide forced her to stop.

As large rocks tumbled down on and around the narrow road, she got out of her car just in time to see someone scurrying away from high above. It suddenly dawned on her that something strange was actually happening out here, just as Clay had insisted. This wasn't an area normally prone to rock slides. At the same time, there was no way she could conceive of Clay being so radical as to go this far. His paranoia had always been more mental than anything else, and he hadn't really had all that much infringement from outsiders. His place was so secluded that few people would ever find it. His activity had been very quiet, that is, it was until they began to travel back and forth so much during the past months. Now the road was much more pronounced, its dirt packed hard rather than the dusty path she had originally traveled on that fateful day last spring. And his mood since the shooting of the animal had been anything but normal. But surely, she remonstrated to herself, she knew this man better than this. They had bared their souls to each other. In their hearts they were married to each other!

In fierce determination she pushed and removed the few big rocks that were blocking her way. But it took her nearly two hours and she was hot and dusty and her hose were ripped when she finished. Still, though, she had only one thing in mind. To find Clay and get some answers and warn him of Jim Reynolds's plans.

When she finally pulled into view of the lane that

led back to Clay's property her heart sank. There below her was a truck from KROY-TV and she knew she was already too late. She stormed up to Mike Carter as he was directing his camera crew into the woods. "What do you think you're doing?" she seethed.

"Getting a big story and without your help too," he said cockily. "I already had the location of this place from the plat records in the county courthouse. We've been out here since this morning and I just found a monitor camera up in those trees so I know this is the place."

"You don't have the right to be here," she said angrily.

"What's all of this?" said an angry voice as both Jessica and Mike whirled around. "Fighting over who's going to get the story first?"

Jessica had never been in the presence of such controlled wrath as Clay came walking toward them, gun in hand. Quickly, before anyone knew what was happening, the cameraman began to tape and Clay's emotional explosion was almost beyond comprehension. "Get the hell out of here," he shouted as he motioned them away with his gun.

"Clay, I don't have anything to do with this," she cried. But her words withered as he gave her the most vengeful, disgusted look she had ever received in her life. Haltingly she brushed her mussed clothes and looked away, trying to avoid the sting in his eyes as she also realized how she must look to him.

"Mr. Farley," she heard Mike Carter in a haze, "would you care to comment on your rather elaborate security precautions?"

151

"Just get off my property," Clay reiterated as he stepped angrily away.

"I don't think we're on your property," Mike Carter went on in his insistent reporter's tone, obviously relishing the nature of the interview. "What are you hiding up there?"

Clay stopped and turned on them in angry silence as his gun hung ineffectually to the side. He was the embodiment of an angry giant about to dispense his own justice. Everyone retreated mentally and physically from the controlled furor of his glance as he leisurely went from one to another.

"Would you care to comment," said Mike Carter, not quite so adamant as he had been before, "on the incidents and harassment that has been occurring around here lately?"

"My God," said Clay as his demeanor suddenly changed and his voice softened. He looked directly at Jessica and seemingly realized for the first time exactly what was happening and all of the ramifications that accompanied it. "I knew there would be something like this after the sheriff's deputy hunted me up this morning, but I never in my wildest thoughts would have believed you would do something like this."

Jessica's heart nearly stopped as she tried to find her voice to cry out her innocence, but something stopped her from even whimpering a protest as she realized she was, after all, responsible for this. She deserved everything he was thinking and saying about her. If she hadn't wanted to do that stupid story last spring, Jim Reynolds would never have taken this direction.

She wrung her hands and turned away as her face and body language told Clay what even he in his terrible and spontaneous anger had not really believed until this moment. He once again took in her appearance, which had always been so special to him in the past. He noted the dirt and smudges and ripped stockings. He was suddenly overcome with both hurt and anger. Everything he had ever wanted or cherished in his entire life was being ripped away from him now in the most heinous of ways, and nothing less than seeing her as hurt and abused as he felt would suffice. "Was the damned story so important," he snarled, "that Miss Superwoman, who has to do everything for herself, would lower herself to physically fight for it?"

CHAPTER EIGHT

"Clay!" she screamed as she went running after him,
unable to keep up with his angry retreating steps. She
stumbled in her high heels and fell to the dirt, coating
the tears on her face with the dust that rose around
her. "I swear to you, this isn't what you think!"

Her voice went through him and touched his soul.
It took every ounce of his strength to deny his instant
protective feelings when he turned and saw her on the
ground. He stood for a moment in great indecision as
his earlier emotions had already cooled to within reason. But as he started to step toward her, Mike Carter
and the TV truck crossed the perimeter of his vision
and Clay knew he had most certainly been the victim
of an ambitious woman one more time. It all made
sense now and this was worse than anything he might
ever have thought could have occurred between them.

"Clay, please," she called as he turned away from
her again. In her panic she had no control over her
words and she grasped at anything, no matter how

inane it might be. "We're going to be married," she cried.

"We are?" he said in absolute amazement as he turned toward her once again. "When did you make up your mind about that? Don't you know enough about me already, or is there even more your conniving mind has to have?"

The pain that went through Jessica was truly beyond endurance and she wondered what terrible fate could make her go on living after this. "I never wanted to hurt you," she said as she broke into convulsive sobs. "Never, never, never. All I wanted was for the rest of the world to know what a wonderful man you are and what you've done for yourself out here."

"I don't believe this," said Clay in continued amazement as his voice took on an air of incredulity. "It's as obvious as it can be, what you've done. You're just another ambitious woman, just like all of those career harpies, and you don't care how you get what you want or whom you hurt. From the very beginning you were after something like this."

"No," she said as she attempted to get up from the ground.

"I should have known," he said as he looked angrily into her eyes and refused to acknowledge the pain and hurt that mirrored through her tears. "What woman would want to live a lonely existence out here? And you come running out here after it and then pull that shy shrinking-violet act when I wanted to get married. All of the ballyhoo over Janey and your family. Why, you're not even above using them when it comes to getting a big exposé."

"Now, just a minute," said Jessica as she finally

155

righted herself and was beginning to feel a little honest indignation herself.

"Oh, don't try to deny it," he said cuttingly. "I've seen how you reveled in being a big news celebrity."

"That's the most wicked, unfair thing you have ever said," she shouted as she suddenly realized how very shallow all of his feelings and promises had to be if something like this could end in such a devastating scene.

"Is it?" he said as he turned and began to firmly walk away. "You haven't heard anything yet. I handled one woman like you and I can do it again."

"Don't you threaten me," she said as she ran after him and pulled him around after angrily grabbing his shoulder from behind. "You may scare everyone else with your gun and big talk, *big man*, but I'm not afraid of you."

The anger between them was hot and fierce and deadly, but even in those incendiary circumstances the very act of touching each other still had an explosive effect. Jessica pulled her hand back rapidly and Clay once again had to force a mental retreat as he responded to the fire and spirit that had tempted him from the very beginning. In forced, almost puppetlike motions they moved jerkily away from each other.

Clay was already beginning to experience a bit of sober rationale as his common sense told him he was obviously the victim of an overreaction triggered by Jessica's appearance here. Never, though, not even in the height of the battle with Clare, had he felt such emotion as this, and never, not with any other woman whom he had been intimately interested in, had something like this struck him such a cruel blow. He couldn't forgive her just like that. That was the way it had always been between them, even when she had admitted deception. He remembered back to that moment in her house when she had told him about being a TV reporter and gnashed his teeth as he remembered how she had seduced him into taping his entire compound and then paid for it by ending up in his bed. That's right, he fumed. Paid for it. Now she would probably go back and play it for all of the world to see and his wonderful peaceful utopia out here in the wilderness would be destroyed.

In the seconds that these thoughts flashed through Clay's mind, though, going from reason to rage again, Jessica had only begun to express her emotions as her anger grew beyond any ability she might have had to control it. Forgotten now were her reasons for coming out here and her own feelings of guilt. All she knew now was that a man who she had trusted and believed in, giving him the very essence of her soul, had turned on her in front of the whole world and made her feel dirty and eternally soiled. She wanted to hurt him as much as he had just hurt her. It didn't matter why or how it had happened. She would never have believed he would do such a thing to her.

"I wouldn't be surprised if you were behind all this trouble after all. You and your fanatical mistrust of the world," she said as she raised her voice so that Mike Carter could hear her from below. "You may have thought you were fooling me when you sent those rocks down on my car, but I know . . ."

"Rocks," he said, as suddenly all of his anger was gone, almost as rapidly as it had come. In an instant he realized why she was so disheveled and it didn't

157

make any sense that two professional reporters from the same TV station would be fighting over the same story. In fact, knowing Jessica as he truly knew her, none of this made any sense.

But she wasn't through as she took another step toward him. "I'm not going to protect you any longer," she said in a deadly voice. "Why should I lose my career and everything I've tried to do for Janey by denying what I know about you?"

"What are you talking about?" shouted Clay as he went to her and forcefully shook her by the shoulders. "Do you know what you're doing to me right now?"

In that instant they both saw that the boom mikes had been taken out of the truck and Mike Carter was busily taking notes as the cameras continued to pan over them. "My God, Jess," Clay whispered bitterly. "You've ruined everything." He pulled away from her, moving resolutely toward the truck. Jessica, in the depths of despair, chased after him, fearful of what he might do. Suddenly her heel caught in the uneven stony ground and she felt herself pitching forward.

Clay swore as he reached out to break her fall, but he was not quick enough. Falling forward, her head struck the hard base of a tree and his words were lost on her. She passed out in a white hot blaze of pain. She knew she had committed the final thrust which would part them forever and she didn't want to hear about it or know about it as she gave into a sublime unconsciousness.

She barely remembered being placed dazedly into her car after Clay had brought her to with a cool cloth he had wet in a nearby stream. He looked carefully into each of her eyes and seemed satisfied. "Here, keep that pressed to your head until we can get you some ice," he said gruffly. "Looks like there'll be a nasty bruise there, but nothing too serious." Mike Carter and the TV crew were gone and there was a firm set to Clay's jaw as he got in the driver's side and began to drive with more than a little determination and conviction. Jessica felt more than a little disoriented as she tried to smooth her ruined clothes and began to experience the discomfort of feeling dirty and gritty. She was just raising her hand to weakly smooth her hair away from the rising bump on her brow when Clay stopped the car with a jerk.

"Is this the rockslide you were talking about?" he asked in a cold, determined voice.

"Yes," said Jessica hesitantly as she tried to fathom what was happening.

"Were you hurt?"

There was a complete lack of care and consideration in his voice as Jessica felt the beginning hint of tears behind her eyelids and she struggled to avoid yet one more indignity.

"No," she said as she raised her chin and refused to acknowledge how much she was hurting.

"Good," he said noncommittally as he avoided her eyes and stomped off.

He was gone for about five minutes and Jessica saw him examine the rocks briefly before he climbed up to where she had seen someone earlier. When he returned to the car he didn't say a word. The silence between them was a shrieking cauldron of emotion bubbling up with malodorous consequences as Clay continued to drive with a quiet determination.

An hour later they were sitting in the sheriff's office,

Jessica with an ice pack on her forehead. "Now I want you to tell the sheriff anything you have to say," said Clay. "What kind of clothes the man was wearing that you saw today. Anything you think I've been up to . . ."

"Clay, I don't understand what you are doing," she said for at least the tenth time since they had pulled up in front of this office.

"I want the right people to know whatever you have to tell," he said with a continued cold determination.

"But what good will all of this do?" she asked as she realized how very real the tragedy was that was happening to them now.

"This thing is going to be splashed all over the papers and TV tonight," he said menacingly, "and I want to be sure the right people have the right information. After some elementary tracking I think I know what's going on out there. I'm going to try to set things straight here and after I'm through you can do whatever you want to with it. But this is the place to handle these things," he ended with a little of his earlier fury. "Not on some damn TV station!"

Stung anew by his words and the terrible things that had just transpired between them that afternoon, Jessica numbly answered all of the sheriff's questions and then turned in absolute weariness to leave about an hour later.

"No, don't go yet," said Clay as he reached out and motioned her to sit down again. "I want you to hear what I have to say."

Jessica didn't question why she followed his instructions. Nothing seemed to matter one way or another anyway as her head throbbed dully and the dead weight of her body slumped into the chair again.

"As you mentioned," he said pointedly as he looked Jessica in the eyes and then quickly glanced away. "I've been spending a lot of time in the woods. Today I think I found what's causing all of the trouble."

Jessica shuffled her feet as suddenly a little of her earlier anger returned. He could have discussed what he thought was going on with her.

"I didn't know what I was looking for," he continued as he met Jessica's suddenly agitated eyes again and then saw the flame die as his words quelled the thrust of her emotions. "But I found a cave out there this morning not far from the rockslide. It looks like someone has discovered rubies in there and they're trying to mine them on a strictly primitive scale. That is government land and they can't stake a claim or buy it, so they're trying to keep everyone else away until they get what they want."

"Rubies!" exclaimed Jessica. "That's preposterous."

"No, it's not," he said as he warmed in spite of himself to the return of color to her cheeks. "These hills around here are full of gemstones—rubies, emeralds, and surely you know about the Arkansas diamonds you can buy in any roadside stand around here. They're mined, you know . . ."

"Yes, of course," said Jessica, "but they aren't real."

"But the rubies are," he said. "I'm sure of it and the sheriff will verify it as soon as he gets an expert out there. I figure now my goat got in the path of some fire meant to scare some campers away."

"So why didn't you tell this to Mike Carter?" said

Jessica as the mortification and shame of that terrible scene rained down on her once more.

"Because I figure it's the sheriff's business first," he answered adamantly. "And, I'm not about to make excuses or defend myself to some idiot who's poking a microphone in my face."

"But it's going to be on the news," she said as she realized that there might yet be another dimension to all of this horror.

"I know," he said. "That's why you're going to call them down at that station now, tell them to send you a crew and microphone and you're going to interview both me and the sheriff. He's had time enough now to get his people out there to protect the mine."

"But aren't you interested in catching whoever it was?" she asked, her reporter's antennae suddenly twitching in spite of all this trauma. Somehow in the back of her mind she just couldn't believe that she and Clay wouldn't get this worked out when they were alone again; and right now she couldn't deny the excitement of getting a big scoop and putting Mike Carter in his place. "If we wait until they come back . . ."

"What about me?" he asked tightly. "Don't you care about all of the damage your little scene out there has done to me today?"

"But it will all be cleared up," she said as her excitement died suddenly when she understood the full impact of his words and she realized her priorities had somehow gotten confused again.

"The sheriff has already thought of it anyway," he said in a final frigid resignation. "I just wanted to see where your loyalties really were."

"What a cheap shot!" she said as once again she was outraged by his behavior.

"Don't worry," he said with a sad, sardonic smile. "You'll get your story. Greed always wins out. They'll catch whoever it is before morning. My instincts tell me they won't be able to resist another haul so long as they don't know we know what's going on."

"And especially since all of the attention is focused on you," said Jessica as everything finally fell into place.

"That's right," he said. "This is good enough to put you into the big time."

"Don't say that," she said as the stark vulnerability of his words finally pierced her and tears came to her eyes.

"What else is there to say?" he asked as he made motions to leave.

"No, please," said Jessica as she was once again aware of all of the people around them. "Let's go somewhere and talk. I'll take you home."

"No," he said wearily. "It's really all over. I knew it from the moment I saw you out there."

"We just need to talk," she said as she dropped her voice to a whisper. "Please come with me," she said. "Let's discuss this in private." She forceably maneuvered his rigid body toward the door and blushed under the gaze of every other pair of eyes in the room.

"Get in the car," he said in resignation. "You shouldn't drive until you've seen a doctor about your head. I'll take you home so you can get cleaned up."

"But what about you?" she asked inanely as again her normal tools of communication failed her. "Are you going back to Owl Hill or what?"

"That's no concern of yours," he said with a sigh. "And it never will be again. Right now all you need to think about is getting the rest of this story and making that moron that was out there today look like the jackass that he is."

A little smile played over her face in spite of her fevered emotions. She was sure she could almost sense the same reaction from him as little ripples of muscles twitched in his jaw. "You do care," she said as she instinctively called upon her oldest ally, her sense of humor.

"Yes. . . . I care," he said as he visibly quelled his droll response. He turned to look her square in the eye. "I care about getting my name cleared and then being left alone. I haven't decided what I'm going to do about what you did to me out there today, but I do know I definitely don't want anything more to do with you. I can't stand any more of this."

"*You* can't stand any more!" said Jessica as she railed against this sudden high and mighty pretension. "I went out there to try to protect you. Do you think this has been a picnic for me?"

"No," he said. "But here we are again. You with your quick tongue and ready excuses and me about to pay the piper for ever caring about you in the first place. This is just one time we can't shuffle it away and say we're sorry. I'm not going to let you touch me like that again."

"Well, when you've learned what it's like to be a human being, let me know," she said snidely.

"It's no good," he said as he stopped in front of her house and they both knew they were aching to reach out and touch each other. "Can't you see? From this point on, all we're going to do is hurt each other."

"Not if we talk it out," she said as she reached out to him.

But he stopped her hand, grasping her wrist almost painfully as he turned away, not wanting to be tempted by something he couldn't deny. "Let it go," he said. "We ripped it to shreds out there today. Now, just let it go."

"No!" she cried as he left the car and began to walk away in silence. "I won't let you leave me like this."

But he didn't stop and in the silence that surrounded her when he was completely gone, Jessica died and yet lived as everything inside her was scalded by her torment. She was barely aware of entering her house and then calling Jim Reynolds. "You made a terrible mistake," she said dully. "And you've also wrecked my life."

The story was a sensation, but Jessica couldn't have cared less because Clay had made himself totally incommunicado and would have absolutely nothing to do with her. It had come down just as Clay had predicted and Jim Reynolds was in no way apologetic for what had happened. On the contrary, this was what he called good reporting and intimated that her loss of professional objectivity was really at fault for her difficulties.

Jessica tried to go back to her work and raising Janey, but the emptiness of her life was almost unbearable. For the first time she was more than sorry that she hadn't married Clay when he had asked her to and she thought often of those promises they had made at the chapel just a few short months before. Janey was also suffering from their estrangement because she had fully and trustingly accepted Clay as a new father. She was beginning to display some bewildering manifestations.

Trying to cope with all of this was almost more than Jessica could handle, and she spent a great deal of time trying to think of some way to get Clay to respond to her. Then in her more rational moments she was genuinely angry and railed against him for refusing to at least make an attempt to work this out. He owed that much to Janey. Over and over again she was assailed by his obvious overreaction toward her and the way he so quickly believed the worst about her. Then she would remember her self-assumed guilt and once again spend half the night crying in her need for him.

It wasn't easy for Clay either. Not a day went by that he didn't berate himself for going so totally wild over the first woman who had interested him since his self-imposed exile in the wilderness. But at the same time he couldn't deny how much he missed Jessica. She was there in his dreams and thoughts; and simple things like the marigolds or a ball game on TV would bring her back. Twice he got into his truck to go to see her, but turned around when he came to the end of his lane and was besieged by the campers who now made this area their mecca since the breaking of the ruby mine story.

In another moment of weakness he picked up the telephone to call, only to have Jessica come onto the TV that now played incessantly, almost as if he needed it to assuage his loneliness. She looked so wonderful—assured and competent. But then he remembered the way she had jumped on that story. He hadn't been all

166

wrong. She had made a fool of him and she had been using him all along.

Ultimately the biggest problem Jessica had was not that she couldn't understand Clay's reactions, even in her more spirited moments when most people including herself would have felt he was being rather pig-headed and unfair about the situation. On the contrary, she understood all too well. In the few months that she and Clay had spent together she had come to know him almost better than herself. She knew the incident with Clare had marked him for life, not just because of the deception involved, although that certainly was a part of it, but because of the bitter self-derision that had occurred as a result of his swift and unmerciless retaliation. Unlike most people, he had derived no sense of satisfaction from his exercise of power. On the contrary, his just vengeance had left him feeling hollow and sick until ultimately he knew he was no better than the other corporate moneymongers he had deplored. He simply could not live with the dirty feelings the situation had created. He had always had a rather rigid standard and as a result of this incident, which was also a smear on his judgment of character, his self-image had been severely damaged. Rather than face the possibility of ever going through such feelings again, he had settled for more modest goals and closed himself away. After his intensive program of mental repair he had made it abundantly clear from the beginning that he held his newfound peace sacred and would guard it at any cost. So Jessica knew very well where he was coming from now, but that didn't make it any easier.

At first she had tried everything, almost shamelessly

throwing herself at him as she tried to call him and then went to see him when she got tired of hearing the receiver click in her ear at the sound of her voice. He was stony and unyielding. The hard, muscular body she had once delighted in was like an impregnable fortress now. It was as if the time they had spent together and the promises they had made had never happened. Jessica had lost count of the many times she had agonized over the memory of the Thorncrown Chapel. Now as he stood before her so adamant and belligerent, Jessica finally realized it was truly finished.

"Welcome to the Farley tourist trap," he said derisively, as he motioned out toward the lane she had just driven up. "I may as well put in water and electric hook-ups and make a quick buck on all of those fools out there looking for more rubies."

"I didn't see more than a camp or two," she said carefully as her eyes tried to break through the cold barrier that shielded his inner emotions from her. "They have the right, you know."

"And you'd know all about that, wouldn't you?" His arms were folded firmly across his chest in unison with the straight line of his mouth as he glared at her.

"Clay, please," she said. "I know a simple apology can't take care of this, but it's not my fault that the rubies were found around here."

She wrung her hands as she took a tentative step forward. She realized that this was going to take a small miracle because among other things it was no longer a private issue between just the two of them. The world had witnessed their tragedy in living color. Then, too, the town had not been particularly kind to Clay initially, which was understandable because of the way KROY-TV had broken the story. Now he also felt he was an unwilling subject of their insatiable curiosity. It would be a long time before he had the total privacy he had once prized.

He stood watching Jessica angrily as everything about her screamed out to him and addressed the lonely longing he was just beginning to find tolerable. He cursed himself for not being strong enough to deny his needs and vowed that he would not make a fool of himself over her again. "I guess you could say that," he answered noncommittally, "but that doesn't change the way it happened, does it?"

"But don't you understand?" asked Jessica as her eyes delved to the depths of his, seeking a crack or tiny weakness, anything that might admit her into the sanctuary of his mind that she had once savored and shared. "You're not the only one hurt by this. Think of Janey. . . ."

"Janey's probably the only one who has ever had this thing in decent perspective." He spoke a bit explosively as he stepped firmly away from Jessica and inwardly flinched from the instant pain in her eyes.

"You're wrong," said Jessica. "She doesn't know what's going on and she feels abandoned. She's starting to do some . . ."

"She'll get over it," he said firmly. "I'm sorry. I don't mean to hurt her, but don't even try to use that on me."

"You're impossible," she said as her voice began to rise.

"Thank you," he answered sarcastically.

The silence was suffocating, like a deadly mantle falling down over them as the vibrations neither could deny reached out and teased in a particularly cruel way. Jessica realized she had made another mistake by coming out here. All she had managed to do was to add another painful memory to her already much too large collection.

"I'm sorry," she said as she turned to go and knew she was going to cry. "I guess I had this image of you. I thought I knew you so well."

Her eyes were blinded with the tears she couldn't control and she nearly stumbled again. Before he could catch himself, Clay was reaching out to her, but she didn't see him as she moved jerkily away. She took a few steps and then stood up straight in a strong, resolute way, willing her tears to recede. Instantly Clay retreated as she turned to face him again.

"You know, I believed everything you said to me," she said. "The promises at the chapel and later at the hotel."

"And I meant every word," he said bitterly as he retreated a little farther from her display of strength and painfully remembered how the hauteur had once been so fascinating. The bravado that supported it was still very much in tact, but he couldn't let her touch him like that ever again. "That's the whole problem," he continued as his voice broke emotionally in spite of his resolve. "I meant it and you didn't."

Her eyes locked with his for a very long moment. Somehow she wanted to record every distasteful detail: the snideness, the belligerence, his haughty stance that accented the tight fit of his clothes in a seemingly mocking way—the way he really was in this moment so she would have something to grasp when she was trying to forget. She wanted to see a man she couldn't love, whom she *could* forget. But it was no use. She knew what was inside that armor. He was in there, the man she loved, but this stranger with his hard resolve and stringent self-discipline wasn't going to let him out again, at least not for her. "If that's what you really think," she said as a weary sadness coated all of her words and motions, "I guess there's nothing more to talk about."

She paused, as if to give him one last chance. She averted her head, but still watched covertly, almost breathlessly, hoping for a sign, something, a reaction —maybe a little twitch in the jaw, a fast blink of an eyelash, or an unconscious extension of his fingers toward her. But there was nothing as he stood in stony, immovable silence.

"Well," she said in sudden contrived exuberance, determined now to salvage what she could of her dignity. She wasn't about to skulk off like some hare-brained wimp. "If you don't mind, I'd like to pick up a few of the things Janey and I left out here. We had a couple of projects we were working on together and now . . ."

"Yes, I know! If you can read a book about it . . ." His voice trailed off as he finally broke his dark silence with one of their old private jokes. Jessica could almost sense a bit of a smile in his words, but she wasn't deceived by it. She knew now he meant to end this and he wasn't going to give her the slightest opportunity to take advantage of even such a small chink as this in that heavy emotional armor he had assembled.

Quickly she moved away with a definite purpose in her stride. She walked up the steps and remembered the first time she had gone into this cabin and the way

Clay had carried her on the day when they made love for the first time. She paused and caught herself beginning to look back toward him, but squelched the impulse, knowing it was useless to even try to recapture the memory.

But as Clay watched her he suddenly knew he was making a mistake. Everything about her, the way she was carrying herself, the courage that brought her here in the first place, reached out to him. Then he saw the sudden set of her shoulders and realized any woman with her spirit and intelligence would rebuff him after the way he had just acted. As the door closed behind her, though, the impulse was quickly diverted when he remembered what loving her had cost him.

Jessica moved about the cabin, touching objects and collecting articles of clothing and craft projects. Over and over again she had to stifle her emotions as she wondered what kind of masochist would put herself through this when it would have been so much simpler to just get in her car and leave. But she was into it now, so she firmly and resolutely continued her task and then marched out to the car with several boxes of items.

Clay had simply stood aside and watched all of this, feeling more and more ineffectual with every moment. It was a beautiful Indian summer day and the sun was bright and shiny on the golden jewels of the autumn leaves that came fluttering down with periodic gusts of cool wind. Finally Jessica felt she had reasonably accomplished her objective and turned to take one last look around. She glanced out across the farmyard to the herb garden she had frivolously planted in the

172

shape of a heart on one of their more glorious days. Then her eyes came to rest on the marigolds, and she remembered the long-range plans they had made for them and felt again a sad betrayal of all their dreams.

"Would you mind," she asked as she deposited the last box and tried to sound as noncommittal as she possibly could, "if I gathered a few of the marigolds? I really would like to knit at least one of the sweaters that they were to be a part of."

Not waiting for his answer, she walked toward the bright bed of yellow flowers. She knelt beside them and realized she needed some scissors or nippers to cut them with. Before she could arise to get them Clay was next to her, handing the nippers to her. She took them from him silently, taking for granted the ESP that had motivated the gesture, while trying to fathom the inscrutable expression on his face. As she bent to complete her task she was surrounded by a sweet and soft aura accented by the yellow and green and gold of the flowers, grass, and trees. There was a sweet tangy aroma of fall in the air and as she brushed her burnished brown locks away from her face there was an appealing concentration on her features that was the epitome of the do or die spirit that Clay had never been able to resist.

Unthinkingly he reached out to caress her cheek and was gripped by a great shudder as the softness of her skin sent him wild. "Woman!" he stormed as he retreated from her startled eyes that had been crinkling with pleasure from the sight of the beautiful flowers. "I think you'd better get the hell out of here before I do something I can't be responsible for!"

Before she could respond he had walked away, surly

and mean. It was almost frightening, and Jessica quickly gathered the flowers together and made her exit. Never would she have believed the intensity of Clay's feelings, which were in reality the exact opposite of his demeanor. In one last emotional battle he had been nearly overcome by his impulse to reach out and crush her to him. As she stooped there in the flower bed, so innocent and revealing in her honest admiration of the beauty before her, he wanted her as he had never wanted her in his life and he knew if he gave in, he would just be starting the agony all over again.

Farley."

CHAPTER NINE

The final blow came about a week later when Jim
Reynolds called Jessica into his office. He handed her
an envelope.

"What's this?" she asked.

"Two weeks notice," he said as he turned noncommittally away.

"What?" she shouted. Unbelievingly she jerked the
interoffice envelope open, tearing it beyond reuse.

"Just what I said," he answered as the terrible look
on her face confirmed his words.

"But why?" she wailed.

"It seems that Mr. Clayton Farley has suddenly decided to withdraw a large number of his clients from
us. There's talk about his going with big city satellite
stations and establishing a business to sell those dishes,
but we know what the real problem is, don't we?"

"No, *we* don't," said Jessica. "What do I have to do
with this?"

"Oh, come on," said Jim as he gave her a disparaging look. "Farley has made it more than clear that he wants nothing to do with anything that has something to do with you. It's as plain as the nose on your face. We can afford to lose you, but we can't afford to lose him."

"Did he actually say that to you?" Her words were laced with fire.

"Well, not in so many words," said Jim, "but the innuendo was clear. Myself, I can't really see him pulling off such a scheme. He needs us as much as we need him, but that's not the way our owner feels and he'd rather be safe than sorry."

"And what am I supposed to do?" asked Jessica as the real implications of the situation finally dawned on her. "Does this mean I can't get a job with any station in the area?"

"I wouldn't know," said Jim with something between a grimace and a sigh. "But for what it's worth, I'm sorry. I don't think you're getting a fair shake out of this."

Jessica was almost numb as she tried to make order out of this. In a final gesture Jim told her to take two weeks vacation to cover her notice time and included a final bonus of vacation pay as well.

Feeling almost naked in her vulnerability, Jessica was livid with rage as she drove home and wondered how she was going to meet her commitments and take care of Janey. Clay had told her on the day that they had their argument in front of the whole world he'd think of something to get even, but she still found it hard to believe he would stoop so low. Then she remembered how he had admitted crushing his partner, Clare, with all of his corporate power. At the same time she remembered that last painful parting and his manifestation of ruthless rage.

In a moment of sheer unadulterated outrage she suddenly knew she wasn't going to let him get away with this. She didn't know what Clare's makeup was, but she, Jessica, was not going to just skulk away or be run out of her own hometown. In a furor she headed her car in the direction of the Ouachita National Forest and was approaching Clay's lane a little while later. She gunned her car and deliberately sprayed dust in the direction of the monitor cameras. "Open your damn door," she shouted. "You're going to talk to me whether you want to or not!"

Clay was completely perplexed by her arrival as her car sped into his drive and stopped with a nasty jerk. He hadn't expected ever to see her again, as he was making plans to sell out and find another, more secluded retreat. Seeing her now with his guard so completely down was almost a happy occurrence as his yearning got the upper hand before he had a chance to retreat.

But Jessica saw none of that as she stormed toward him. "How dare you try to take my livelihood away from me," she seethed. "I almost hope you are this petty so I won't ever waste another thought on you, but I'm not going to let you do this to me without some satisfaction! I'll sue you if I have to."

He was a picture of exasperation as he looked at her. "What in God's name are you talking about?" he asked as he tried to fathom what demons had taken possession of her mind and body.

"Oh, you . . . you low snake in the grass," she said gutturally. "Don't try to deny that you're threatening to take your business from the station if I continue to work there."

"I don't have to deny anything," he said as he stepped toward her and felt his own ire beginning to rise. "All I'm doing is preparing to get the hell out of here and go someplace else where I can have my business and my retreat too. This place is an absolute zoo since you pulled your shenanigans out here."

She gave him a snide look. She wasn't having any of this. "Is this what you did to Clare?" she asked as she lowered her eyes and gave her voice a low, cynical twist. "Is that why you hate yourself so much that you have to hide out here in the wilderness?"

She flipped her head menacingly and looked him straight in the eye. She was possessed with a furor so strong that there was no room for softness or conciliatory emotions. Yet, the simple sight of him so close to her in the same room was suddenly shocking, bringing back full force all of the familiar responses she had to him. She couldn't allow herself the luxury of such feelings now as she watched him wilt before her and a sly insidious thought began to form in her mind.

Clay couldn't deny the pain her words caused, but with each barb she convinced him only that his initial reaction to retreat from this relationship since the day of their estrangement had been right. As she raged in front of him, for whatever reason she felt justified it, he firmly closed the door on caring. He was in a bit of a haze as he heard her strident voice continuing to berate him.

"If you can't stand to be near me or even be indirectly involved with me, I'll fix you now. I'm coming out here with my Brownies, all twenty of them, and

I'm going to camp right on your doorstep until I hope you go crazy from the sight of us!"

Clay was incredulous as he realized what was actually happening here. "Jessica," he said as if to calm her. "I don't know what's happened to you, but I honestly didn't have anything to do with it."

"Do you expect me to believe that?" she asked. "Did you believe me when I said the same thing to you?"

"But this isn't the same," he reasoned as he realized how insane her proposal was, and knowing her she would try to do it. "You can't involve those kids in something like that."

"Why not?" she said as she looked at him and tried to deny that he was reasonable or appealing in any way. "You didn't have any qualms about upsetting Janey. And besides, we've worked on this all summer. What difference does it make where we camp? You said yourself there's always plenty of company out here now."

"You've got that right," he said as he looked derisively down the lane. "But I think whatever is going on, we ought to talk about it."

"Oh, you do, do you?" said Jessica in perfect magnanimity. "Well, it just so happens that *I* don't feel like talking with you anymore. All I care about is aggravating the hell out of you and you can count on my doing it! Maybe then you'll wish I had a job to go to instead!"

He shook his head as he watched her in amazement. Obviously there was no reaching her now and in spite of all his well-secured reserves concerning his own emotions for her, a little smile began to play around his lips.

Jessica saw it and was immediately drawn to the devil in his eyes as she realized he was laughing at her. It was the final straw. He wasn't going to get her fired from her job and then laugh about it too. She *would* dedicate herself to doing her damnedest to drive him nuts. She could feel an uncomfortable blush creep over her body as he looked at her now with that same quizzical mischievousness he had displayed when she was trying to pitch her tent on the day they had met.

"I'll do it," she said. "So help me God, I will."

He looked at her for a long time. He wasn't retreating now. It had been a long time and he finally couldn't resist the honest reactions she fired in him. "This I've gotta see," he said softly as he infuriatingly scanned her from head to toe, reveling in her heaving breasts and the thrust of her pouting lips.

"You will see," she said flippantly. "And remember. I know exactly what drives you nuts!"

She left him then and Clay realized she had gotten to him. Her fire and spirit and bravado tinged with that ever so familiar sense of comedy had gotten to him where sentiment and yearning could not. It was ridiculous. The whole thing was ridiculous and he realized in all good conscience he had to set this straight before she did something that was more foolish than anything else she had ever tackled. He remembered the ball game now and all of the many other times they had laughed together. She was dear and funny and he was a fool to think he could deny his feelings for her any longer. In the end peace without love and laughter wasn't worth having.

He took care of his chores and then he got into his truck and started toward town. He was hoping she would have had time to cool down, but when he arrived, Jessica was already in the process of organizing the camping trip.

"Look, Jess," he said as he approached her in his most conciliatory, but nevertheless firm voice. "Don't you think you'd better rethink this? I'll go with you tomorrow and get whatever is wrong straightened out."

"Ah-ha!" she shouted, still very much the victim of her angry, erratic emotions. "I've really got you going now, haven't I? Just the thought of twenty little kids out there messing everything up drives you wild, doesn't it?"

"What drives me wild," he said as he grasped her by the shoulders and inwardly reveled in the very feel of her, "is the thought of someone getting hurt or . . ."

"Don't worry," she said cuttingly. "You won't be responsible, and take your hands away from me."

She removed his arms from her shoulders and valiantly tried to quell her racing heart and the loss of breath his touch had generated. Visibly she tried to ignore the raw, potent virility that had always accompanied his rugged countenance.

"Jess, I came to talk. I know I haven't treated you well."

"Oh, you don't say?" said Jessica as she lowered her voice calculatingly. "When I was out there groveling at your feet I should have thought of this threat."

"Don't be ridiculous," he said as he felt his patience slipping. Couldn't she see how hard this was? Why did

181

she have to feed the feelings that warned him about giving in to his emotions like this?

"It's too late," she said as in sudden realization she understood it really was. After the way he had treated her and refused to even talk or say a decent comradely good-bye to end the relationship, he wasn't going to just waltz in here and say, Guess what! I've had a change of heart. Leave the Brownies home and let's kiss and make up!

He saw all of these thoughts play over her face and knew exactly what she was thinking. "Don't make the same mistake I did," he said as his eyes became hypnotic beacons of appeal and he reached out to touch her again.

"I wouldn't think of it," she said as she pulled away from his embrace and the brush of his lips on her own, and instantly had to fight a rampaging response. "Now, go away and leave me alone," she said weakly. "I have a lot to do to get ready."

"You can count on it," he said as he walked away in a huff and she allowed the screen door to slam with a nasty snap when she stomped into her house.

She had more than enough anger and frustration to carry her through the next few hours, but she soon began to feel honest remorse as she realized she had botched it with Clay again. On further examination it seemed that she was more the victim of the station owner's paranoia than Clay's maliciousness and she, in her wild anger, had thrown away the first opportunity to communicate with him since that terrible day when Mike Carter had recorded their rift. She wasn't surprised that Clay didn't try to follow up his initial attempt at reconciliation. That just wasn't his nature, given the circumstances.

Her plans for the Brownie camping trip suddenly seemed a silly, futile gesture. Even after all the time she'd spent up at Clay's retreat, she knew she was not yet experienced enough to handle twenty or more children out in the wilderness. Now, in a rational state of mind, Jessica didn't know what had gotten into her. How could she dream of possibly endangering the children just to satisfy her own spiteful whim? Clay's visit had taken its toll on her emotions. It seemed she dropped from an energy high of white hot anger to a feeling of mournful exhaustion. There would be no trip to Clay's Owl Hill. There would be no vengeful scheme of retaliation. Clay was probably innocent, as he claimed. Not that it would do her any good to try to tell him that she believed him and was sorry for her accusations.

As Jessica dropped into bed in an exhausted heap, her last thought was that she had truly thrown away any last chance for reconciliation with the man she would always love. Once, she had believed that their strange meeting and undeniable need for each other was destiny. She had believed with all her heart that she and Clay were two halves of one whole, meant to be united for all time. Now she didn't know what to believe. She knew only that Clay was gone from her life, never to return.

CHAPTER TEN

Jessica slept fitfully, her dreams filled with images of Clay. She woke in a cold sweat in the middle of the night, calling his name and was filled with a deep sense of loss compounded by the terrible conclusion that their love was never meant to be. On impulse the next day, she left Janey with her grandmother and then set out for the ultimate catharsis. With a few overnight things packed in a small case on the backseat of her car, she left her mother's home with a real sense of mission. For too long Clay had preyed upon her mind and now she knew she had to do one last thing before she could let him go for good.

It didn't take long to arrive at Thorncrown Chapel, and as every mile sped away Jessica could almost envision the pain that she was about to experience. But she had to go back where the sacred promises had been made. She had to relive them and examine them one more time to discover how they had been flawed. Maybe then some of the ugliness since that time would make more sense and perhaps she would be able to live with the reality that she now fully understood was, indeed, reality.

As she walked up the familiar lane with its cherished memories her heart nearly stopped when the chapel came into view. Wisps of the warmth and love Clay had so willingly and naturally extended to her in her time of need came hurtling back, drowning her in confusion and longing. Suddenly the stillness of this reverent place was shrieking and the sounds of the woods became cruel taunts. Dazedly she wondered what masochistic force had compelled her to come here as she stumbled on in unbearable agony. In one last desperate gesture she delved deep, searching for some redeeming reason as all of her emotions welled up, and she knew her torment was too great to contain. "Clay!" she cried as her body convulsed into hunched grief and she made no effort to control her tears. "Oh, Clay, Clay, Clay," she sobbed as her anguished call echoed through the woods.

So great was her grief that she didn't hear the nearby rustle of fallen leaves. Clay's voice was soft and deep, a perfect reflection of the love in his eyes as he answered her appeal. "Did I hear my name?"

Jessica whirled around, afraid to believe what she had heard.

"I knew if we were really destined to be together, you would come here," he said as he walked toward her. "I've been waiting for a very long time."

"Oh, Clay," she cried again as she ran into his arms. "I'm so tired of being so stupid about so many things."

"That makes two of us," he said as he pulled her

185

into a warm embrace and brushed her tears away. "What do you say we go back to the very beginning and start with something simple like I love you."

She nodded happy assent, her tears flowing, as the sun streamed through the trees and glanced from the chapel windows down over them. Never in her life had she had a happier moment. They stood in happy communion, feasting on the sight of each other as Clay's lips met hers hungrily and Jessica closed her eyes in sweet euphoria, knowing she and Clay would never part again.

The wedding, a few days later, was small and simple but everyone attended who was important to them. Now, as they snuggled in each other's arms in a small white-water raft that was floating serenely down a sparkling cold Colorado stream, Jessica was sure that her serenity could never be destroyed again. As their fingers trailed in the rushing water Clay reached over to kiss her and then jerked to attention.

"Get ready," he shouted. "I can hear them coming up."

"Oh, no," shouted Jessica in a panic. "I'm not ready." She reached for the rafting book as Clay hastily positioned her in the rear behind him.

"Forget the damn book," he shouted as the roar of the rapids grew noticeably louder and he handed her a paddle. "If you aren't ready, it's too late now."

The words whipped out of his mouth as they rounded a bend and the raft dipped deeply into the cold water and then went whirling down through the frothing torrents. Skillfully he used his paddle to ward off the rocks while Jessica tried desperately to emulate him.

186

"You said you wanted to try this," he shouted. "You knew you could do it."

"I can do it," she shouted back. "Just mind your own P's and Q's." Her voice was filled with a mixture of excitement and exultation tinged with just a hint of panic as the water washed over them and the raft dipped savagely, whirling about like a crazy carnival ride.

"Whooee," shouted Clay. "Keep her steady, we're almost through."

The words were barely uttered when there was a sudden disastrous drop accompanied by a drowning deluge that washed both of them out of the raft.

"Clay," called Jessica as she righted herself and tingled from the exhilaration of the cold water. She had been hurled into a much calmer pool at the end of the rapids and felt instant relief when Clay's arms went around her and she reveled in the feeling of his lips on hers as he kissed her with wild, intense excitement.

"What fun," she said, laughing as they salvaged the raft together, pulled themselves up on a grassy shore, and felt the weight of their soggy clothes and life preservers.

"You liked that, did you?" said Clay as he responded warmly to the excitement in her face and pulled her close to kiss her again. Then they savored the aroma of the pine forest as their breathing slowed to normal and their fingers entwined naturally together.

"So what are we going to do now?" she asked as she tugged on his ear with her teeth and then leaned back to relax and bask in the rays of sun seeping through the yellow poplar and aspen trees so splendidly arrayed in their autumn colors.

"How about getting dry for starters," he said as Jessica looked at him in amazement. "Come on. You know I always come prepared." He grabbed her hand and began walking up into an obviously secluded glade, producing a shiny compact blanket, matches, and several tins of wine from his deep inner vest pockets, all well protected in a heavy plastic covering.

"You never cease to amaze me," said Jessica as she traipsed happily after him.

"I know," he growled as he pulled her close and began to help her out of her jacket. "Let's just say I've grown very accustomed to these antics of yours."

Their eyes met and they laughed as they felt their bodies melding together in a happy familiar fusion. Clay quickly started a fire and then mischievously assisted Jessica in removing her wet clothes. Their fingers touched when Clay handed her a tin of wine and they snuggled together, savoring the warmth of the fire which the iridescent blanket magnified and reflected on their bare bodies. They were ecstatic as tiny nibbles and teasing explorations slowly built and ignited into the wild intensity they had never been able to control. Laughing, Clay pulled her close, while his lips followed their familiar path down her neck and found their quarry when they encircled the rosy nipples of her breasts. Gasping in pleasure, Jessica took another sip of wine and then reached to nip his earlobes, delighting in the tangy mixture of wine and flesh.

"Ouch," yelled Clay as she deliberately added the salty taste of blood to her sensual concoction, only to

188

arouse him to higher piquant peaks than he had ever experienced before.

"Vixen," he growled as he pulled her beneath him and devoured her naughty lips and clashed with her stinging teeth until her parrying tongue bowed in wild submission. His hands moved over her body, teasing and touching, seeking out all of the familiar intimate places while she performed her own brand of magic, which left him gasping with pleasure when her hands completed their teasing and he brought his strength to her own bed of desire—but not before his fingers moved swiftly through her thighs and brought her perilously close to a glorious peak.

In wild abandon he rose above her and titillated her with soft tiny thrusts before he plunged to the depths of her body and delved in wild, roaring excitement for the satisfaction they both craved. In the brisk air their bodies gleamed from the exertion, but they felt only the heat of their desire which was now, and always would be, out of control. Jessica exulted in the pungent aroma of the woods, the soft moss beneath them, and the distant roar of the water below. It was a fitting accompaniment for all of their emotions as she looked into Clay's eyes and reveled in the pounding strength of his masculinity. With a wild cry she joined him in their crescendo and savored every word of love that poured from his heart as their bodies quieted together and she felt the last tiny pulses of his spent desire in sync with her own happy rhythms.

"We're crazy," she said as they snuggled together in the blanket again. "What are we doing out here when we have a luxurious honeymoon suite to go to?"

"I guess it just goes with the territory," he said,

189

laughing. "When you're married to a crazy woman you end up doing crazy things, but I'll tell you," he added as he nibbled her ear, "I can stand a whole lot of crazy when it's like this."

"Mind your tongue," she said conspiratorially. "I wasn't the one who dumped us."

"Oh, no!" he said as he suddenly couldn't resist her bait. "I'm not the one who bought the book and then said in her sweet, appealing voice, 'Let's go rafting, Clay.'"

He had added a comedic mincing to his words which Jessica found hilarious as she buried her face in the hair on his chest and pulled him close again. "Maybe so," she said as she tightened her arms around him. "But I'll tell you one thing. I was sure glad to see you when I came up for air."

"I told you from the very beginning," he said huskily as he turned her face up and looked deeply into her eyes. "Just call my name and I'll always be there."

Her eyes were shiny as he again swept her into his embrace and Jessica knew that was one thing she would never doubt again. He was her hero and he would always be there to protect her whether she needed him or not. "I love you," she whispered, "more than anything in the world."

No other words were necessary as he answered with his own intimate response, and they once again sailed to the heights of a brand-new euphoria as only they could create it together.

LOOK FOR NEXT MONTH'S
CANDLELIGHT ECSTASY ROMANCES®:

CANDLELIGHT
Ecstasy Supreme